The Chest of Visions
Secrets of Caperston

The Chest of Visions
Secrets of Caperston

TIM FERGUSON

Foreword by Frank Tangredi

Illustrations by Jose Carlos Gutierrez

RESOURCE *Publications* · Eugene, Oregon

THE CHEST OF VISIONS: SECRETS OF CAPERSTON

Unless otherwise indicated, Bible quotations are taken from the Good News Bible.

Resource Publications
An Imprint of Wipf and Stock Publishers
199 W. 8th Ave., Suite 3
Eugene, OR 97401

www.wipfandstock.com

PAPERBACK ISBN: 978-1-7252-7960-5
HARDCOVER ISBN: 978-1-7252-7961-2
EBOOK ISBN: 978-1-7252-7962-9

Manufactured in the U.S.A.   08/20/20

To Christian youth,
who have asked honest and challenging questions
as they grow in a faith which makes
a difference in the world.
You are the leaders of the world.
May your faith bring the world together in Christian love.

I will pour out my spirit on everyone: your sons and daughters will proclaim my message; your old men will have dreams and your young men will see visions.

—JOEL 2:28

Contents

Foreword

I've known Tim Ferguson for 45 years. And there have only been a handful of people who have influenced my life more.

We first met in 1975. I had just returned home after graduating from college. He was leading a young adults Coffeehouse in the basement of the local Presbyterian church. Most of us who came to the Coffeehouse regularly saw it as a social organization—a place to have fun, make friends, maybe even meet someone special. (A lot of marriages, including my own, came out of that group.)

But Tim always envisioned it as something more. It was his way of doing God's work and doing something to improve the community in which we lived.

That was still Tim's mission a few decades later, when he started running the church's Youth Group out of that same basement. I eventually became his assistant and got to witness firsthand how his vision was really bearing fruit. This, I could see, was what Tim was really born to do.

The fun was still there; that's why the Youth Group attracted many kids from outside the Church. But now Tim had a chance to do more teaching. He was always trying to find new ways to bring the word of God to our youth. New ways, too, for our youth to do God's work, especially feeding the hungry.

It was out of this quest that The Chest of Visions was born. It's a highly imaginative mingling of Christian theology and modern scientific theory (something else that has always fascinated Tim.) It takes the story of Jesus and re-imagines it on a different world with a different set of characters. But it isn't a simple retelling. Just when you think you know exactly where it's going, it hits you with a surprise that packs a powerful emotional wallop.

Tim wants to give youth a fresh perspective on Christ's message—and he succeeds.

Today, Tim and I are still friends. He is still dedicated to mission work and community outreach. And he is still teaching, this time one of our Confirmation classes. (He can't stop. It's in his blood.)

I'm teaching the other Confirmation class. In fact, I'm now chair of the Christian Education committee. But I wouldn't be doing either if I hadn't walked into that basement 45 years ago. Tim is still influencing my life. When you read and use The Chest of Visions, he may influence yours.

Frank Tangredi

Preface

The story of The Chest of Visions began with an effort to bring the gospel in a creative way to a junior high/high school youth group in Deer Park, New York. We had been corresponding with a young lady on a year long mission trip by posting monthly letters we received from her on our Christian Youth website. The youth enjoyed keeping in touch with her in this manner.

Then her mission trip ended. After meeting with her upon her return from the trip, we went our separate ways. Since the youth enjoyed the monthly letters, a decision was made to continue a similar correspondence on the website, this time with young people residing in a faraway land, in fact, in another universe. It was the universe of Caperston where no one had a concept of God.

Letters from the faraway planet captivated not only our youth but many adults, who were visiting the website on which they were posted. Someone suggested combining the letters into a book and that encouragement was all that I needed. Then the idea of writing the gospel story, as if it happened in a different universe, emerged.

I remember reading a story of a mythical being when I was young. It was a relatively short story but what made it captivating were the illustrations that helped me visualize the story. A contact with the illustrator, Jose Carlos Gutierrez, found him enthusiastic about the project from the very beginning

Published initially in 2012, a continuation of the story was written several years later. Wipf and Stock Publications expressed interest in that story, "The Chest of Visions: New Pathways 'cross Broken Highways," but also wished to pick up the publication of the first book.

The Chest of Visions: Secrets of Caperston is now a revised version. What has changed? Some reviewers, who offered positive critiques of the book, expressed an interest in knowing more about the youth and adults of Caperston. In response, this revised version follows the initial plot but offers more details about the individuals, who follow Chihaysu as well as some, who oppose him. This revised edition also gives details about the customs of Caperston, similar to many customs on Earth but with differences, in part, due to only recently experiencing the concept of the existence of a God.

The revised version also has two additional lessons, for a total of twelve, for youth group leaders to use as youth read the story of Caperston in the Chest of Visions series.

Acknowledgments

I would like to thank my wife, Linda, for her continuous support while I worked on this project. I want to thank my sons, Scott and Brian Ferguson, for reviewing the initial manuscript of the book and making helpful suggestions. I also wish to thank my friends, Frank Tangredi and Davina Durgana, and my wife, Linda Ferguson, for their review of a revision of the book and for their comments.

A special thanks is given to Jose Carlos Gutierrez for his inspired artwork throughout the book and on the front cover. Jose's prayers for the project and his enthusiasm encouraged me to continue to develop the story as well as the characters of the youth of Caperston.

Lastly, I want to thank all of the young people I have worked with over the past forty years. Their enthusiasm for truth and questions about matters of faith challenged me to find a creative way of presenting the gospel message.

TIM FERGUSON

1

In the Beginning

In the beginning there was God . . . so reads Genesis chapter one.

In the beginning there was a singularity. So states the theory of cosmology, the study of the origin of the universe. This singularity was infinitely small, made up of the most elemental of atomic particles. These particles were in constant motion and their location could not be identified. In a sense they were nowhere and yet everywhere.

About fourteen billion years ago a gravity-defying force appeared and the singularity exploded in what is known as the Big Bang. The universe expanded to about the size of a grapefruit then split into several identical universes. Just as human twins grow up genetically identical, yet different as they mature, so did these universes. For our story we simply consider two: our universe and the universe of a young man named Mattpaul.

Mattpaul's world evolved simultaneously as the world of Earth evolved. In some ways we on Earth are more advanced. In other ways Mattpaul's world is. One thing is clear. Mattpaul's world of Caperston has been the more orderly world until recently when new emerging ideas began to challenge age-old traditions.

It is important to understand that Mattpaul's planet is much smaller than Earth and revolves around a smaller star. It is closer to that star and makes many more revolutions over a given period in time than Earth does. For example, during one earth year, Mattpaul's planet makes 50 revolutions. Thus, twenty- five Earth years would equal 1,250 revolutions around

Mattpaul's star. With such high numbers of "years" passing, Mattpaul's world measures time by the generations that pass not by the actual years.

One last introductory fact must be mentioned. Contact from Mattpaul is due to their development of Strings technology, a recent innovation in his world of Caperston. In Appendix One the science behind Mattpaul's ability to communicate is discussed.

In Appendix Two there are three approaches youth leaders can adopt if they choose to use the book as a study guide. Appendix Two also contains twelve lessons that can be used in discussing the story. It is recommended that youth leaders review these lessons prior to having youth read the story.

For now, let us begin our journey to Caperston through the eyes of a faraway friend from a different universe. Let's hear Mattpaul tell his story.

2

Getting to Know You

Hello,

Are you there? I am reading your electronic news. You mentioned a book, the Bible, but I am not familiar with it. Is it a holy book? You also talk about Christian youth and the man Jesus. I would like to learn more. I am not sure how I found your news report. It seems to have been by accident. I put some numbers into my compol, and your report appeared.

My name is Mattpaul. I live with my parents a short distance from Lake Gael in Caperston. I am in my last year of school and I look forward to completing school and beginning work. My father is an assistant to our Ruler and has promised me an important job when I graduate.

We live comfortably and never have worries. We are called the Valley People. There are some rich Valley People, who are fortunate and live on the shore of Lake Gael. It is pleasant to visit their homes. Even though my father is second in command, we live more modestly. That is fine with me.

There are also Mountain People, who have much less than we do. We rarely see them except for our annual kickuml contest. They live on the other side of Lake Gael in older residences. They appear to be friendly, and I want to get to know them better.

I went with my teacher and class to visit the Mountain Village and discovered that their world is different than ours. They live higher in the mountain where it is colder, and they wear more modest clothing. They

grow their hair longer to protect them from the cold. Our teacher said that
Mountain People have lived on the mountain for many generations. No one,
not even our books, talks of a time when the Mountain People came down
from the mountain except to fish in Lake Gael. After fishing they immediately return to their villages. Once every ten days or so, one family member
comes into town to gather supplies. Sometimes they pay with denorites and
other times they barter with fish.

The occasion for our visit was a kickuml game against the Mountain
Youth. We thought we were good but a little while into the game a ball was
kicked high in the air. Before it landed a Mountain Youth jumped up and
struck it with his head. Our goal protector was so surprised that he was slow
defending the hit and it became the first goal of the game.

We never saw someone use his head in this game and asked our coach.
He checked the rules, which said that we cannot use our hands, but nothing
is listed about using our heads. So, the game continued, and the Mountain
Youth were particularly good at using their legs and their heads. We lost.
After the match, a Mountain Youth named Marcus offered to teach us how
to "head" the ball. We listened and practiced this skill with him. We will
learn it and maybe do better the next time we play.

My friend Huchfee and I spoke with Marcus after practicing with him. He told us of a man who has visited the village. I do not know how to spell his name, but it was pronounced: Chi-hay-su. This man talked about another ruler who did not live with us but was everywhere. Marcus said that Chihaysu was going to speak at a meeting place on Lake Gael in a few days. Huchfee said we should leave school to hear him speak. I do not know.

I could get in much trouble, but I would like to go. Perhaps I talk too much. I hope someone gets this message. If you do, write, and ask questions.
Mattpaul

DATE . . . APRIL 30TH

Dear Mattpaul,

You did not leave a contact e-mail so all I can do is add some thoughts to your correspondence. Your letter and my response will be recorded on a webpage, which, when you visit again, you will be able to read.

I am not sure where you live. You give an address of Caperston. Is that a country? Is it a town? You also mention a compol. What is it? I would like to learn more about the differences amongst your people. Thank you for telling me of the kickuml game. It is very much like a game we call soccer. Lastly, the Bible is a holy book. Have you ever read one? I would like to get to know you better.

Tim

DATE . . . MAY 2ND

I am glad someone read my message. Lake Gael in Caperston is my address as our world is small. Caperston is my country. You asked about my compol, but first let me tell you my story. Huchfee and I were worried that we would be caught when we went to hear Chihaysu, but we were not. On the day he was visiting, our teacher cancelled class and gave us a project to complete. We left but did not do the project. We figured we could do it later.

We left school and walked around Lake Gael to go where Chihaysu was speaking. He was sitting on a piece of wood beside the lake. There was a group of about fifteen individuals, all adults except for Huchfee and me.

Chihaysu talked about someone named God, who is like our Ruler. He said our Ruler oversees our world, but this God rules over our feelings inside. He also said that our Ruler treats the Mountain People differently than he treats us, the Valley People. Chihaysu claims God treats everyone, Mountain People and Valley People, equally because our feelings and our dreams are the same.

Mattpaul

This idea excited me. When I talked to Marcus last week, I felt like him because we had many of the same hopes and dreams. In addition, we are the same age.

I also really liked when Chihaysu taught us how to talk to this God. It is something he calls praying. This was an unknown activity to me. Chihaysu insisted that everyone be quiet and, at first, I was uncomfortable with the silence. Then I began to feel peaceful. Since Huchfee and I were afraid of being discovered, we could not stay long so we quietly left. We then went and completed our project. Huchfee went home but I sat down and looked across the lake. It was a nice day. Then I tried the praying activity. I was not sure that I was doing it right, but I am glad that I tried.

Is praying an activity which you do?

You asked about my compol. It is a communication device. In our third year of school we are all given a training compol, which is used in our education. All our tests and assignments are given on the compol as well as music and some comedy shows. It was on my compol that I reported on my project a little while ago.

After our sixth year in school we are given a new and better compol, which allows us to do additional things. There is a station with news of everything that is happening in Caperston. My father often appears on this news station. We also now have the ability to send messages to friends and family members. After we write, we place our thumb on the screen signaling that the message is completed. It was in my experimenting with my compol that I found you.

I hope I will get a chance to hear Chihaysu speak again. He was interesting.

Your new friend,
Mattpaul

DATE . . . MAY 3RD

Dear Mattpaul,

Thank you for describing your compol. Now I understand. Chihaysu talks about a ruler, whom we also know. We call him God. Chihaysu's teachings remind me of a person, who we believe was God's son. We are told this man, who lived many years ago, was named Jesus.

You ask about praying. Yes, it is an activity we do. It is both difficult and easy. It is difficult because we do not know where to start. When I am in church, I hear our pastor pray with such ease. Words flow out of his mouth as he talks to God. Then there is time for silent prayer, and I am unsure of myself.

However, prayer is also easy. When we realize that our creator, God, cares enough about us that he wants to hear from us, well, then it is like talking to my best friend. God is our friend, Mattpaul. Your friend and my friend.

Please continue to write.

Tim

DATE . . . MAY 8TH

Dear Tim,

I am excited to tell you this. Chihaysu came to Lake Gael again, closer to our village and many people came to hear him, including my father, my sister Rachaeling and her friend Michaeling. He spoke about a ruler, whom he also calls God, and then told a story that I keep thinking about. It was something like this. There was a man who was traveling across Lake Gael when his boat hit an underwater rock and began to sink. The man was far from the shore and could not swim. Fortunately, he managed to pull a piece of wood from the boat before it sank. He stayed afloat by holding the wood.

A short time later a powerboat was seen in the distance. The man waved for help. The boat was driven by one of the Ruler's most important advisers. He lived in one of the fancy houses on the shore of Lake Gael.

The advisor slowed down as he approached the man and called out, "I am sorry my friend; I cannot help you as I am already late for a meeting with the Ruler." He quickly drove away leaving the discouraged man holding onto his piece of wood.

Several hours passed and the man was getting cold. He tried kicking his feet to stay warm when another, smaller powerboat appeared. It was driven by the leader of the school. In his boat was a large fish which he had caught earlier in the day. The driver saw the man and steered his boat to him. He reached into the water, touching his hand, but realized that the only way he could pull him into the boat was to discard the prize fish he had earlier caught. He sadly looked at the shivering man in the water and stated, "Friend, I am so sorry. I have never caught a fish this size and need to bring it home and have it stuffed so it may be displayed in my den. I am sure someone else will come." He then left, leaving the cold man behind in the water.

It was almost dark with the only light coming from a sunset. The man in the water was ready to accept his fate when he heard a "Swish . . . swish" from behind him. A Mountain Man was paddling towards him. When he arrived, he reached over and pulled the man to the side of the boat. Then the paddler realized that the only place he could sit was behind him and that seat was covered by a large bucket, filled with small fish. The paddler stated, "My friend and brother, you are from the valley and I am from the mountain. I have been fishing all day, making a good catch, and my family will be well fed this evening. However, God has brought me here to you and you are more valuable than any, in fact, than all of these fish." With that said he emptied the bucket of fish into Lake Gael and pulled the man aboard, paddling him to safety.

What a beautiful story Chihaysu told. It makes me think of what I would do if I were driving a boat towards this man in the water. Chihaysu asked, "Who was the truest of friends?" We all called out, "The Mountain Man." Chihaysu replied, "Stop being separate from the Mountain People.

In God's eyes you are all equal. Reach out to them and make them your friends."

My father told me that the man Chihaysu seems to be an inspirational man, but that he does not understand that we and the Mountain People are simply different. But I remember Marcus. He was just like me and I want to be his friend.

Mattpaul

DATE . . . MAY 11TH

Mattpaul,

Thank you for sharing your story. I think others would like to hear it so I will feature your letters on my home webpage. I hope we will find interested youth from our world to correspond with you. I also hope you continue to make an effort to see Chihaysu. He seems to be a good man and is asking people to open their minds to working together as equals.

It is a message people in our world also need to focus on.

Tim

3

Who is Chihaysu?

DATE . . . MAY 19TH

Hi Tim,

I am sorry for not writing for a while. After the meeting with Chihaysu, we asked our schoolteacher about him. Is he one of the Mountain People? He does not really look like them but neither does he resemble a Valley Person.

The teacher said that a generation ago the Mountain People were dispersing into different villages. This dispersion was beginning to move northwest towards an uninhabited area known as Stone Woods. The Ruler asked them to come to the valley to register so he could understand where they resided. The Ruler was nervous about this expansion into an area not far from the homes of the Valley People.

This registration had an impact. Many Mountain People met and decided it was best to move back together towards the mountain region. There is now one major village and three smaller ones. The Ruler was extremely pleased and considered the registration a success. There is a rumor, my teacher said, that Chihaysu was born during this time of registration and, since it was an unstable time, it is unclear who his parents were.

Chihaysu has not appeared at Lake Gael since I last wrote. We, particularly the Valley Youth, hope to see him again.

Your friend,
Mattpaul

DATE . . . MAY 26TH

Greetings,

Let me share more information. Though we have not seen Chihaysu for a while, our teacher told us something interesting. He said there is a rumor that Chihaysu visited one of the small communities on the northeast side of the Lake Gael. All the communities are having trouble with a disease called AHT. This disease makes people feel dizzy and tired, falling into a sleep that can last all day. We have medical equipment to diagnose diseases in Caperston, but this disease is new, and the equipment has yet to clearly diagnosis the ailment and a cure is, therefore, unknown.

The rumor is that there was a girl, named Dawnling, who had the AHT disease for many days. She is a year away from completing school and her cousin is Marcus, who taught us how to "head" the ball in the kickuml game. Chihaysu told her parents to pray to God for healing.

They asked Chihaysu to pray with them and the next day she was better, no longer feeling dizzy and tired. Our teacher said that this suggests that praying may do more than to bring peace to the person praying. If the rumor is true, prayer may result in God intervening to make things better.

I look forward to learning more about what happened. I am sure someone will ask Chihaysu the next time he visits us. Huchfee heard that he is coming to Lake Gael in a few days.

Mattpaul

DATE . . . MAY 30TH

Dear Mattpaul.

My name is Alex. I live on Earth and, while searching the Internet, I discovered Tim's website and your letters. I really appreciate how honest you are. You tell us not only what has happened but how you feel about it. I envy you. You have met Chihaysu and heard him speak. We only know of our Jesus by what was written about him. I love your stories.

Please keep writing and sharing. When something happens of interest here on earth, I promise to share it with you.

Alex

DATE . . . JUNE 7TH

It is nice to meet you Alex,

Hopefully, this message will arrive. I tried two times since my last letter, and it appears the messages did not go through. So, I worry.

Chihaysu did visit Lake Gael a few days ago. My father asked me to go and take notes. So, I went with Huchfee. When we arrived, we found my sister, Rachaeling, and her friend, Michaeling, already present. Michaeling told me that, after she heard the boat story, she thought that it was a story everyone should hear. She asked me about my visit to the village, the kickuml game and what I thought of their youth who hit the ball with their heads. I said, "They won and did not break the rules." Michaeling said that in kickuml they were smarter than we were and maybe we can teach them things we know, and they can do the same. My sister was listening and, when we finished, she whispered something to Michaeling then winked at me. Michaeling seemed very interested and, besides, she is pretty.

Chihaysu talked about the Mountain People. They built their houses into rock, often the side of the mountain. Then he spoke of the Valley People, who build their house on the shore of the lake. Their homes are beautiful, but when the winds blow and the storms arrive, which house is safer? We all said, "The Mountain House." Chihaysu said that building a house into the mountainside is like living your life with God holding you up. When storms of life come, God is there to keep you strong. Others depend only on themselves. They are like the house on the lake. When difficulties come, there is no support for them.

Michaeling asked Chihaysu how we can get support from God. Chihaysu reminded us about prayer and believing that God can provide us courage when needed. I asked about the young woman who became healthy after prayer and Chihaysu said that we should never doubt the things God can do.

That is an idea that I like. So does my sister, Rachaeling. I am glad she brought her friend Michaeling.

Mattpaul

4

My Conflict

DATE . . . JUNE 11TH

Hi again,

It is me. Alex. Once again you speak of the young woman, who became well after prayers were said for her. It seems there are many young women, who seem interested in Chihaysu's teachings. Here on Earth there is one particular young woman, who has a strong faith. Her name is Laura and she is the youth leader of our Youth Group. The adult leader is our pastor. He is young and we all relate to him because he has much of the same energy that we have. Laura is a friend that I know I can rely on. She is not a "girlfriend" but a friend who I trust and whom I call talk to when I need someone to listen.

I have something important to share but first I have a question. Perhaps it is silly but do all of the women in Caperston have names that end in "ling." Their names are very long compared to women's names on Earth. It is probably not important but then I thought, maybe there is a reason for this.

Now to the important matter.

It is a good thing that Dawnling got well after the period of prayer. However, my recent experience has not been so good. We have been told that God cares about us. If he does, why did he let one of my best friends, Kevin, die?

Kevin was working on a mission project with our youth group. We were feeding homeless individuals and so many people came that we ran out of plates. Kevin went to a store a short distance away. Ten minutes later we saw four police cars heading towards the store. An ambulance followed and I ran to see what happened.

When I arrived they were placing Kevin into the ambulance. The police told me that he was an innocent victim. They are not sure what actually happened. While Kevin was purchasing the needed plates, a robber entered the store. The storekeeper pulled out a gun for protection. It seems that he randomly fired missing the robber and hitting Kevin in the neck. The storekeeper claimed that he fired when the robber attacked him but another observer disputes this. The police were more focused on getting treatment for Kevin. They apparently did not arrest the robber but took information from him for a future investigation.

Kevin died before reaching the hospital. He was a good friend and faithful follower of Jesus. Why did God allow this to happen? You speak of the goodness of your God, but I think of God as being uninvolved and not fair. How could he allow a good person, like Kevin, die?

Our pastor met with us the day after Kevin was killed. He had no answers except to say it was part of God's plan. What kind of a God would have a plan that included a young man, who was helping the homeless, be killed?

You are lucky. You have Chihaysu to whom you can ask questions. I have explanations from my pastor, but it is not the same. I wish I could ask Chihaysu my question.

DATE . . . JUNE 26TH

Alex, my friend,

I appreciate that you share from your heart. I am sorry about your friend's death. Why would God let good people die? This bothers me too. I have been so excited about Chihaysu's teachings that I assumed only good would come to his followers. I will ask him your question for you.

Now let me tell you a little more about Caperston and about Chihaysu's last visit. Our family has lived here for twenty-two generations. Our ancestors were the first to move here and lived in the valley near Lake Gael. There were others already in the area. They were the ancestors of the Mountain People who live northeast of the lake. From the beginning the Valley People felt superior to the Mountain People. Their houses were better furnished even having electricity, which the Mountain People still do not have to this day. Within four generations the Valley People became rulers over the Mountain People. It happened because the Mountain People wanted things that our ancestors had and willingly submitted themselves to the Valley Ruler.

Our community is small. There are many homes, a few shops in which to purchase goods and the House of the Dead. It is the largest building in Caperston and is only open on special holidays when we can visit our deceased relatives. However, only Valley People can be buried there. Mountain People are not considered to be worthy of such a distinguished burial place. They bury their dead in caves on the north side of the mountain.

There are two types of burial places in the House of the Dead. Those, who lived well, have a decorated tomb where relatives can easily see their graves on visiting day. The second type of burial is for criminals, who are dropped into a large hole in the ground with no grave marker. Their only recognition is the listing of their name in a book in the front of the building. Overseeing the House of the Dead is an important job that pays very well. The current overseer is retiring in a couple of years and my father has picked me to work with the overseer after I graduate. If I do well, I will soon have this prestigious job.

Our Ruler has many rules that tell us what to do. However, Chihaysu teaches that God has just two laws. The first is to love him because he created this world and looks after it. The second law is also about love. We are to love the Mountain People the same way we love our own Valley People. Why? It is because God loves us all equally. Love is something that we youth think about a lot. Huchfee even told me that, overall, he thinks the Mountain Girls are prettier than the Valley Girls. However, he did admit that there is one Valley Girl who is very pretty. I asked him, "Who?," but he will not tell me.

What do you think? Does your holy book have a similar teaching?

Mattpaul

DATE . . . JUNE 29TH

Dear Mattpaul,

Thank you for writing and telling me more about your world.

You asked about the teachings of our holy book. It teaches that God loved our world, and, because of this love, he sent his son to it. This son was named Jesus and Jesus chose to become human and become one of us. He did this to understand what it was like to be human. There was also a second reason. He came to Earth to give his life so that our wrong actions can be forgiven. One of his followers, named John, wrote an accounting of Jesus and his teachings. John stated that Jesus came into his own country but that many fellow citizens did not believe his teachings. However, some did, and they received the right to be children of God.

Later John wrote in one of the best known segments of our Bible, John chapter three verse sixteen:

"For god loved the world so much, that he gave his only Son, so that everyone, who believes in him may not die but have eternal life."

Another follower, Matthew, talked about a time when God will judge everyone by their lifetime deeds. Those who reach out to the poor, the sick, and the imprisoned will be rewarded. Why? Jesus said that whenever we do something for the poor and the needy, we do it for him. He became human so that he could understand our human feelings, our joys, and our pains. I am so glad that Alex has been writing to you. He has been struggling with his faith and you have been so encouraging.

Tim

DATE . . . JULY 7TH

Dear Alex,

I asked Chihaysu if God would allow a good person to die and why. Chihaysu replied that there was a young man named Jonton, who a generation ago spoke out against treating Valley People and the Mountain People differently. Jonton challenged Valley People to change their view. He was arrested and never seen again. Some thought that he was murdered and tossed into the pit with the criminals at the House of the Dead.

Chihaysu stated that, when he learned of Jonton's fate, he wondered why God would allow this bad thing to happen. He appreciated Jonton's willingness to speak out even with the threat of danger and, when he began to teach similar ideas, some people remembered Jonton and told him that they were glad Chihaysu was raising these ideas again. Jonton died but was not forgotten. Perhaps Kevin will also be remembered for his good deeds.

After telling me the story of Jonton, Chihaysu walked over to a group of children. He said that true faith in God was like the faith a little child has in his or her parents. A child does not doubt his parents and, when a parent asks a child to do something, he responds. Likewise, Chihaysu says we should react to God's guidance.

Like your Jesus, Chihaysu reminds us to reach out and help the poor and those facing troubles. There is a man who acts differently than most of us. He is older than my father but acts like a child. He says that he hears words from the trees, which tell him what to do.

Michaeling saw him and said he looks sad and lonely. She tried to speak to him, but he hung his head and walked away. Most people walk away whenever he approaches, but Chihaysu says he is a person in need and

God wants us to love him. Huchfee, Michaeling and I agreed that the next time he appears, we will ask him how he feels and if the trees have told him anything recently.

Mattpaul

DATE . . . JULY 8TH

Hey Mattpaul,

Thank you for speaking to Chihaysu and telling me the story of Jonton. Perhaps, instead of being angry, I will think of ways to honor Kevin. Perhaps Kevin's death will bring us all to a realization that we must reach out to those in need.

I have not been in church since a short time after Kevin's death. My parents, who always insisted that I go, understand. They said it is my decision to determine when I am ready to return. I am not ready. What I really wish is that I could live with all of you in Caperston.

Alex

5

Teachings

Greetings.

I told you about the man who talks to trees. We saw him the other day and went to speak with him, but he replied, "Not today, not today." He then pointed to the crowd that was gathering to see Chihaysu. He climbed up into a tree so that he could see and hear but so that no one would know he was there. Huchfee stated that he seems afraid of everyone. We will try to befriend him again.

My friend Marcus was present with his cousin, Dawnling, and her parents. I walked over to join them, and Marcus introduced me. I asked Dawnling what she felt when she was ill with the AHT disease then got better. She said that she had slept for several days, waking only for brief moments, mostly to drink some water. She does not remember Chihaysu coming but remembers waking up and feeling like her illness was a dream. The next day her parents told her of Chihaysu's visit.

Dawnling is convinced that her parents' prayer with Chihaysu led to her recovery. She concluded: *"faith does not just believe. It takes action."*

Dawnling explained, "Listening to Chihaysu speak is one thing, but actively praying is taking an action of faith. When we hear the Word of God from Chihaysu, we must say 'yes' to it. This is what faith is—'saying yes' to the Word of God. I came today because I hope to learn what I can do for others as God has helped me."

We then heard Chihaysu speak and this time he talked about fisher-
men. It was a good topic for all of us as the people of Caperston are mainly
fish and fruit eaters. Up to eight generations ago, we ate meat from animals,
but our doctors warned that this was dangerous. So, the Ruler declared that
eating meat was illegal and the fishing industry became very necessary.
When Chihaysu started talking about fishing, everyone listened.

For some reason I wondered about the "Man who talks to trees." I
turned towards the tree he climbed and, there he was, not only listening but
writing on a pad of paper every time Chihaysu paused in his presentation.
Was he taking notes? I do not know, but he seemed very attentive. Maybe
when he said, "Not today, not today" what he was saying is, "I am here to
listen to Chihaysu." The next time we see him, I will ask him what he thinks
about Chihaysu's message.

Chihaysu then surprised us by saying that he was not talking about
fishing for fish but fishing for people. He challenged us to speak to our
neighbors and friends about his teachings. Soon he will begin recruiting
some helpers, and anyone interested must make a full-time commitment.
Huchfee and I looked at each other. We will soon graduate from school, and
my father expects me to begin working with the overseer at the House of the

Dead. If I tell father that I wish to become Chihaysu's helper, he will say I am being foolish, but I am extremely interested.

After Chihaysu stopped speaking, instead of returning home, we followed him. He walked quite a distance to Lake Gael and then knelt and appeared to pray. He bowed his head for a few seconds then looked to the sky. We did not hear him say a word, as we were a distance away. We remained for quite some time and then quietly left so as not to disturb him. Chihaysu, apparently, likes to visit quiet, beautiful spots to relax and pray.

Mattpaul

DATE . . . JULY 27TH

Mattpaul,

Chihaysu is looking for helpers, you say. Full-time? I wish I could be with all of you. If I lived in Caperston, I think I might sign up.

There is something about Chihaysu that energizes me. I assume this is how people felt when they met our Jesus, two thousand years ago.

Alex

DATE . . . AUGUST 12TH

Dear Alex and Tim,

Huchfee and I graduated from school. There was a short ceremony and most of the townspeople showed up, even those who did not have children graduating.

In Caperston graduation includes some recognition for not only good students but for students who are particularly helpful to the community, even though it was not required of them to do so.

My friend, Huchfee, won an award for offering to work with a daily newsletter. This is a brief overview of events happening in Caperston, events in the Valley and the Mountain Villages. Events like the birth of a child, building a new home or winning an athletic contest are included. Huchfee's job was to visit and take down notes which he would bring to the editor. The newsletter is usually one to two pages long and is made available every morning at a stand in front of the House of the Dead. It is called "The News of Yesterday, Today and Tomorrow." Why tomorrow? On most but not all days our learned scientist calls in a forecast for the weather he expects for the coming day.

Another friend, who graduated with us, Michaeling, won an award as the "Most Caring" Graduate. She was recognized for taking time each week to offer to read to a group of our elderly, whose eyesight was going bad. Three days every week, after school, Michaeling went to the home of Ms. Bette, whose husband died a half generation ago. Ms. Bette invited three elderly friends, two women and a gentlemen over to listen to Michaeling's readings. She would start by reading from the "News of Yesterday, Today and Tomorrow," then continued with a longer story the participants chose. Michaeling told me those in attendance a week ago could not agree on the new book to read. The gentleman wanted a story about a fisherman, who caught a prize fish. Ms. Bette stated that she wanted a story about a child that dreamed about the future. The other two stated that they would listen to either. So Michaeling reads about the fisherman on one day then the next day she reads about the child, who dreamed. My friend Michaeling is, indeed, a special person.

I am glad both Huchfee and Michaeling got rewards. They deserved it.

A few days later Huchfee and I walked partway around Lake Gael to where Chihaysu was speaking to people interested in being his followers. He told a story, but I need to explain something first. Here in Caperston we have animals that live with families. We call them goadas. They are friendly, four legged animals that are very obedient. My parents have shared that, if my sister and I would obey the way our goada obeys, then everything would be easy. But we are young and sometimes we think differently than our parents.

In Caperston no one can bring a goada into their home until the goada is fully grown. So, from birth until full growth the goadas are raised by people we call goaderds. It is hard work as the goadas reside outdoors. Only when the goadas are fully grown are they introduced to living indoors.

Chihaysu told a story of a goaderd, who was watching his goadas. There were 100 goadas he was responsible for. One night he counted ninety-nine coming into the pen to sleep. He was upset.

He told his assistant to watch the ninety-nine goadas while he looked for the missing goada. His search lasted until the next morning and, when he still had not found the missing goada, he returned to the flock. His assistant told him that bad things sometimes happen even to obedient goadas. The goaderd spent the rest of the day caring for the remaining ninety-nine goadas. But that night he could not sleep. He got up in the middle of the night and looked in an area he had missed the night before. It was difficult but, when morning came, he heard a whimper. He turned towards the sound and there, standing on a rock ledge and terribly frightened, was the missing goada. The goaderd picked the goada up and ran back to the herd. There was rejoicing that the missing goada was found.

Chihaysu concluded that those of us, who would like to be his followers, must be like this goaderd. We must remember the importance of all, who are in need. My father says that there are only a few poor people in Caperston and that they now reside in poor houses and are given one meal each day to eat. Father says that we should thank the Ruler for solving the problem of the poor. Chihaysu does not agree. He teaches that there are people, who are poor in spirit because they do not understand that God loves them, and that God wants them to pray to receive inspiration.

I like this story, particularly when, even as he was encouraged to focus his attention on the remaining ninety-nine goadas, the goaderd did not forget the missing one. That missing goada was important to him, and we need to share God's love even with those who do not realize that they are lost.

I think I want to apply to be a follower of Chihaysu. My friend Huchfee said that he is not ready to be a follower. He is not sure if he will come to the next meeting with Chihaysu because he feels it is only for those who wish to be Chihaysu's followers. I wonder how many will return.

Mattpaul

DATE . . . AUGUST 13TH

Awesome . . . that is what this story is. The goaderd did not give up on the lost goada. He found him and brought him to safety.

Why didn't God protect Kevin like the goaderd protected his goadas?

Thank you for sharing about Huchfee and Michaeling's recognition at graduation. But what about you, Mattpaul? I will bet that you received some recognition too.

Alex

6

Becoming a Follower

Hi Alex,

A few days ago, I met with Chihaysu and seventeen others who were interested in becoming his followers. We were at a beautiful garden and from it we could see the center of Caperston. Huchfee did not come with me but one of the Mountain Youth, Marcus, was present.

You may remember Marcus. He was the Mountain Youth who taught us about "heading the ball" at the end of the kickuml game. Marcus is an excellent kickuml player and, in fact, scored two goals against us in our annual match.

What I really like about Marcus is his honesty. He graduated this year, not from our school, but from the Mountain School. He also got an award for "Most likely to Succeed" in his class. I can believe that. Marcus is not only smart in his mind; he speaks well and is motivational, just like Chihaysu. I look forward to getting to know Marcus and I am sure that Chihaysu is pleased that he is thinking of being one of his followers.

Chihaysu did something very interesting. He asked us to walk with him. We walked to the shore of Lake Gael down a pathway off the main road from the Mountain Village to the Valley Village. Along the way Chihaysu stopped, picked up a flower and said, "Look at this flower. How beautiful it is. Every morning when the sun comes up, it reopens to show us the orange and red within. Then at night, it closes up to rest. God, our unseen ruler, created this flower and cares for it. It is why I call God our Caring Creator. If he can care for a flower like this so carefully that he makes sure it gets its rest each night, will he not care for every one of us. Remember this flower when your worries trouble you. We have a Caring Creator."

I love this story. To know our creator cares about us, even though he is unseen, gives me a feeling that God will protect me. But then, I understand, there is the case of Kevin on Earth. Why was he not protected? I think I will ask Chihaysu again, "If God protects us like he cares for the flowers, why did he not protect Kevin?

When we arrived at Lake Gael, Chihaysu told us he needed to pray. He could not keep all of us as his followers and needed God's guidance in choosing. He encouraged each of us to pray then walked away. All around there was silence and, for some unknown reason, I became afraid where my mind might wander. Would weird, perhaps evil thoughts, emerge? An event from my past kept coming to my mind.

A schoolmate of mine named Zester had invited some friends and me to his house. He asked us to be quiet and said he would call for a ghost to make itself known. I replied, "What is a ghost?" Zester grinned. He told us a man was killed while living in the house and, in the quiet of the night, you could hear the man moaning. I was scared and Zester said we should count our heartbeats to ourselves, all the way up to twenty-five. My heart was pounding. A short time later Zester said, "Do you hear it?" I heard nothing, but most of the others said they heard moaning.

As we left my friend Huchfee stated that he did not hear anything, but Lucius, another friend, said he thought he did. Huchfee said sometimes people can put an idea in your head and you will imagine things that do not exist.

So, this night in the garden, after Chihaysu walked away, at first all I could think of was the ghosts that possibly lived in the garden. Then, re-membering what Huchfee said, I recalled Chihaysu just said, "Pray." He did not say, "Close your eyes, pray and you will hear God." So, I decided to try to pray.

After a few moments, I opened my heart and ask God to speak to me. Calmness replaced my fear and a peace came over me. Shortly afterwards I thought of Marcus. It would be good to have another youth join Chihaysu with me. I am glad he is considering being a follower of Chihaysu.

I was feeling peaceful when Chihaysu returned. I knew nothing of the others, but I heard Chihaysu say, "Seven of you are sleeping, not praying. We have challenges ahead and I need followers who will ask God for as-sistance through prayer." He asked the seven to leave and said to us, "You, who prayed while I prayed, will be my followers. Go home and prepare to join me in a few days for the journey that will be ours."

One of those, who prayed and did not sleep was Marcus.

Tonight, after I write to you, I will speak to my family. Your friendship, Alex, gives me hope, as I fear that my father and even my mother will not be pleased.

To answer your question. Yes, I did get some recognition at the graduation. They used to give an award for the graduate who was "Most likely to Succeed," like Marcus received at his school. This year they did not give this award and said they decided to call the award, "Most likely to Make a Difference." It is the award I received, and I am thankful for it. Why they changed the name of the award, I do not know.

Mattpaul

DATE . . . SEPTEMBER 1ST

Alex,

A while ago you stated that you wished to be in Caperston. Sometimes I wish that I could live on Earth and have a family like yours as your family supports you and lets you choose to believe or not to believe.

Last week, when I spoke with my father, he was upset that I am postponing working at the House of the Dead to become a follower of Chihaysu. He said that Chihaysu wants to change things that do not need changing and claims that Chihaysu does not respect what the Ruler has accomplished.

I tried to explain that Chihaysu tells us to be thankful for what the government has accomplished but that there are still people who are poor in spirit and who do not know that they are spiritually empty. They do not know what prayer is and how fulfilling it is. They go about their lives doing assigned tasks and never ask why they have been given these tasks. They do not try to understand that God wants to be a part of every person's life. They do not even understand that there is a God who exists. The idea of a Caring Creator is something my father cannot consider.

Chihaysu teaches that the Mountain People are more open to the presence of God than the Valley People are. I understand what he means because of the day I prayed. While I prayed, I opened my mind to God and asked that he give me new understanding. I received a sensation of peace at that moment which was amazing.

I do not know what is going to happen. Father will not even discuss what Chihaysu has taught. He rejects him as a troublemaker. I know it will be hard, but I will commit myself to follow Chihaysu. I spoke with my sister Rachaeling, who told me she overheard my conversation with father. She seems to understand, and I think she is a secret follower of Chihaysu, but I am not sure. Mother is sad. She listens to me but says father is her husband and she must support him. She said that she knows I must follow my heart.

I want to share one more thing. My father is a good man. He is wise and he is humble. The Ruler, Pontos, could not rule effectively without my father taking his directives and bringing them to the people. I am proud of him and I know that he and my mother love me. It saddens me that, although being highly intelligent, my father does not see the emptiness we feel inside in Caperston.

I wish I knew how to share what I have experienced with him.

Alex, Tim . . . do you have any suggestions?

I will be leaving to join Chihaysu in two days. It may be more difficult, but I will find time to write. Your support is valuable and the words you share give me encouragement.

Mattpaul

DATE . . . SEPTEMBER 3RD

Dear Mattpaul,

I first want to congratulate you on your award, "Most likely to Make a Difference." We never know what path God leads us down, and I am sure that God has a special plan for you in Caperston.

You ask about reaching your father. The first thing I would suggest is to be consistent and patient. When God calls us, we have an assurance in God's call that goes beyond any confidence we have in other decisions we make. Your father will see that assurance and respect you for it.

Secondly, the chief difference between a believer and a nonbeliever is the condition of the heart. Your worries about your father are evidence of your true commitment to the calling of God, in your case through the ministries of Chihaysu. Keep your faith and bring your father to God in prayer. As you have said, your father is a good man and God recognizes that. Through you, Mattpaul, I am confident that your father will eventually come to believe. Maybe that is why you received the award for "Most likely to Make a Difference." A difference in your father's life.

Tim

DATE . . . SEPTEMBER 8TH

Thank you, Tim

Your thoughts soothe me. My father is a caring man and it hurts when he will not listen to Chihaysu, whom he once described as "inspirational." He closes his mind when I try to tell him how following Chihaysu has changed the way I see our world. I always felt that Mountain Youth and Valley Youth were equals. Now I feel that I have a mission to share that belief with others. Maybe this is the "difference" I am supposed to make?

Mattpaul

DATE . . . SEPTEMBER 14TH

Hi Mattpaul,

I am sorry that I did not write to you after your August 25th letter. I am a bit confused by a recent event in my life here on Earth. My friend Laura called me and said that the youth group at church missed me.

I then asked her if she really believed in God. She stated that she did. I questioned how she could believe in a God, who would let Kevin die. Laura said that, after Kevin died, our minister spoke to the youth group and stated that God predestines certain things in our lives. I asked Laura what "predestined" meant and she explained that our minister said that God decided his plan included Kevin dying during that robbery.

"Why?" I questioned.

Laura replied, "Alex, I do not know. I believe in God, but I troubled with a God, who would plan for a good person like Kevin to be killed in an accidental shooting. It makes me wonder about the use of firearms by those not trained to use them."

Now I am really upset. Not only did God let a good person like Kevin die, he planned it. Believe me; I am ready to give up on this God idea all together. Even Laura cannot change this feeling. But Mattpaul, your story, your honesty, your faith, all these things keep me wondering. Please continue to write.

Alex

DATE . . . SEPTEMBER 22ND

Hey Alex,

It looks like you have found support and understanding from your friend Laura. She seems to be honest and a good listener.

I wish I could be with you but all I can do is write and pray for you. I understand the reason you feel as you do. If Huchfee was killed, particularly in an accidental way, I would feel the same way.

Let me continue to tell you of the events here in Caperston. I spoke with my father one more time. He listened then said, "You are of age so just go." As I left, I walked to the shore of Lake Gael with my sister, Rachaeling.

There I met another follower of Chihaysu, Jonas.

Jonas is older and has a family. His wife is named Laura, just like your friend Laura, and he has a baby son. Jonas was the very first person to express an interest in following Chihaysu. Like me, he had made friends with Mountain Youth after a kickuml game several years ago. He still meets with them to talk about kickuml contests which, over the years, have always been close. One of his Mountain Friends is a fisherman and, every time Jonas visits, his friend sends Jonas home with a small bucket of fish. Jonas states that his Mountain Friends are very caring and generous people, even though most have low paying jobs.

Jonas has taken some long trips, up into North Woods where he thinks he saw some giants roaming the woods, but he is not sure as the sun was going down and it was getting dark. He says he wants to go exploring again but, for now, he has a family to support and take care of.

Jonas has a special skill. He is an artist and has done wonderful draw-ings. He showed me a few and I asked if I could try to send one to you. It is of Chihaysu speaking to our people on the day Huchfee and I skipped our afternoon project to hear him. Let me know if you get the picture.

Rachaeling was going to walk me partway around Lake Gael then re-turn home as she had some chores to do. When Jonas heard this, he stated that he had a friend, who offered to sail both of us across the lake with him, saving much time. Rachaeling encouraged me to do this and turned to return home.

Jonas and I agreed and climbed into his boat. As we began to sail away, I saw Rachaeling was joined by her friend Michaeling and they both waved goodbye. It made me feel good and I returned the wave.

Jonas, his friend Levee, and I left. The weather was genuinely nice, at first, but suddenly it became windy. The waves turned white and our boat was rocking. Levee is a skilled sailor, but he was having trouble controlling the boat. We were afraid as we were in the middle of the lake. Jonas and I held on to the side of the boat with one hand.

Finally, Jonas called out, "God, save us." At that moment I could see a figure in the distance. The figure appeared to be standing on the water.

It looked like Chihaysu. I called out, "God, help us." The figure then waved his hand to the sky and slowly the winds lessened, and the waves became smaller.

Sometime later we sailed safely to the opposite side of the lake and saw Chihaysu sitting on a large rock at lakeside. He said that he saw everything, the sudden wind, the high waves; he even heard someone call out "God, help us." Chihaysu said that, when we sincerely call out to God, God responds. God caused the winds to calm when, by calling out to him, we demonstrated our faith.

Later that day Chihaysu taught us that we are just starting to learn the things of faith. Our faith, though small at first, will grow to become powerful.

We have a large tree in Caperston and Chihaysu took a seed that fell from it. He said, "See how small the seed is and now look at the great tree that has grown from it. Your faith will grow to be large like this tree." He taught us that, in this way, we are similar to the tree but, in other ways, we are much different. The tree has no consciousness. It does not think. But God made something great out of something so little. What can he do with each of us if we genuinely believe and act upon our beliefs?

God has blessed us all with an awareness of ourselves and the world around us. For this reason, he calls us to work for the good of the world he created. This is our responsibility. I feel this responsibility includes working with my friend, Marcus, and hopefully others to reduce the lack of equality between Mountain and Valley people. It just seems to be the right thing to do.

Mattpaul

DATE . . . OCTOBER 1ST

Mattpaul

Wow! What a story! God caused to storm to subside when Chihaysu raised his hand. Chihaysu raised his hand after hearing you call out God, help us. That was a prayer.

I believe I also need God's help, but I do not know how to ask for it. I do know this . . . I want to be with you in Caperston.

Thank you for Jonas' picture of all of you with Chiyahsu. He is quite talented, and it is good to see what you all look like. I can tell which person is Chihaysu as he is talking in the picture. Which person in the drawing are you, Mattpaul?

Alex

DATE . . . OCTOBER 4TH

Dear Alex,

Let me answer your question in your last letter. Chihaysu is on the log speaking and Huchfee and I are behind him. Huchfee is on the left and I am to his right.

After meeting with Chihaysu, following the storm, we travelled with him and his followers. He taught us so many things that I cannot share them all. One teaching that I think about a lot is this: we are all lights for this world to see. We need to let God shine through us so that people can see in our faces the loving people God calls us to be. Whenever I pray, I feel an energy building up in me that I hope is radiated out for others to see.

At a Mountain village someone asked Chihaysu where he came from and did he have a family. Chihaysu replied that we, his ten followers, are his family and that anyone else, who hears the teachings of God and who follows God's teachings, will become his family. We all felt special when he told us we were like a family.

Tomorrow we will go out, two by two, apart from Chihaysu for the first time to share the many stories and teachings he has taught us. I will be speaking at a school to young people like myself. I am uncertain if I am ready for this and my companion, Marcus, is just as uncertain. Amongst Chihaysu's followers, he has become my best friend.

I will pray a lot tonight and hope that the light, which Chihaysu promises will take over us, will shine tomorrow as I speak to the young people.

Mattpaul

DATE . . . OCTOBER 8TH

Dear Mattpaul,

This is Tim. I want to thank you for continuing to be an inspiration to Alex. I pray that God will turn that light of faith on in you. Our Jesus once stated,

"You are the light for the whole world . . . No one lights a lamp and puts it under a bowl; instead he puts it on the lamp stand where it gives light for everyone in the house."[1]

This is what you are doing right now, brightening all those who encounter you with your energetic, youthful faith. I believe that one day your father will truly see, not only your faith, but the value of the love you demonstrate for your brothers and sisters, residing in the Mountain side of Caperston. What a special place this would be, your world and our own, if we took time each day to fill ourselves with God's spirit and to let it shine wherever we go.

DATE . . . OCTOBER 14TH

Tim . . .

Thank you for your kind words. Marcus and I discovered that speaking to the youth at the school was not as difficult as we feared. Most of them seemed interested. However, one called out, "We do not want any Valley People here. You treat us as inferiors but now you preach love to us." At first, I did not know what to say. I almost cried because I have never felt that way.

I let the boy speak. When he stopped, I replied, "I can imagine how you feel but Chihaysu tells us that God sees everyone as equal and so do I." Another youth stood up and said, "You talk about this man named God. Why does he send you? Can he not come and speak to us himself? Where does he live?"

I was uncertain how to respond. I looked to Marcus. Marcus' cousin, Dawnling, had just arrived and, when he saw her, Marcus became energized and spoke confidently. "No one knows where God lives," he explained, "but God is all around us when we pray." The boy replied, "How do you know?" Then I told him the story of the storm at sea when I called out for God to help us and the winds stopped. The boy responded, "Nice story, Valley Boy; I will have to think about it."

Marcus replied, "Faith is not easy. It has troublesome moments. My cousin, Dawnling, can tell you how God healed her, and she is now ready to help others as she has been helped." The boy listened, paused, and said, "It is good to hear a Mountain Youth talk about this God."

Dawnling, a very shy cousin of Marcus, was a good but quiet student in school. She is one year younger and lives with her parents as their only child. Her father, like so many other Mountain People is a fisherman. Her mother is one of the schoolteachers at the Mountain Lower School.

---

1. Matthew 5:14–15

In the Caperston we have two schools. One is for the younger children who learn to read and write and learn about numbers, how to add and subtract. There is also physical education, running, jumping and kickuml. We all loved this part of our education. Two other fun things we did were music and acting. Acting is part of our reading classes. We would have parts in plays and would act our role as we learned to read our lines in the play. It was great fun and at the end of the school year there would be a school show followed by a cookout with our favorite foods. Everyone would join a chorus to sing in the end of the year concert and the best readers get to read skits in front of the audience. I got to be a reader in two of my five Lower School years. Almost everyone in town comes out to see the performance.

For the older children there were other subjects added including personal health. We also had a work assignment to learn to be responsible in terms of completing our duties and being on time. The best students would get an opportunity to take more challenging classes which their parents paid for. There were four years in our Upper School.

Dawnling's mother was voted best liked teacher the last two years in a row. Dawnling told Marcus that when she grows up, she wants to be a teacher, just like her mother is.

Dawnling stated that Chihaysu had helped her but that she did not really want to talk about it at this time. There would be another time, just not right now. This was acceptable to the Mountain Youth and they asked her to share with them when she was ready to do so. Marcus and I walked her back to her home.

Then we left, feeling good about the day and I think we will be ready to go out again. Maybe someday I will speak to the Valley Youth. Maybe Huchfee, Michaeling and my sister, Rachaeling, will hear me.

We returned to Chihaysu, who asked everyone how our day went. Jonas and his partner said that they spoke to groups of fifty, perhaps more. They were all adults. Another follower stated that his group of listeners included the banker of Caperston, who seemed interested. Marcus spoke for us and stated that we spoke to twenty young people. Everyone frowned upon us until Chihaysu thanked us and stated, "It is the youth who will change the world."

I asked Chihaysu the question raised by the youth about where God is. Chihaysu said that, although we cannot see him, he is everywhere. He does not live in a structure like we do; rather he lives in the hearts of all believers. I think I now understand. God is the light that shines out of me when I pray. I like that thought: God is light; he is the entity that brings brightness to the world. That is what I will say the next time I am asked the question about where God lives.

I know, Alex, that you see darkness when you think of God at this time, but he does bring light. Kevin was God's light in your world.

Mattpaul

DATE . . . OCTOBER 18TH

Mattpaul, my friend,

I believe that you feel the presence of God in your heart. We were taught that his spirit lives within us. At this time, I find it hard to let his spirit in, but your kind words and stories encourage me.

I trust that the Mountain Youth will respond positively to the message Dawnling, Marcus and you shared with them.

Alex

7

An Inoculation of Hope

DATE . . . OCTOBER 24TH

Alex:

I am glad my stories encourage you. The other day Chihaysu was teaching about faith. Our faith will be tested. We are being sent away for three days to share Chihaysu's message. We are not to worry about what food we will eat and where we will sleep. God will motivate the hearts of people to take us in and feed us. Chihaysu said we should not take food or money with us. "Have faith," he says, "God will provide for you."

I am anxious, as this is a long trip. We start at Lake Gael on the south side and begin by travelling to five different locations amongst the Mountain People. This time Jonas will join Marcus and myself. We will stop at the first village and discuss Chihaysu's message then invite everyone to a special speech he is making. Then we travel north, and it will be a day's journey, where we repeat the same message at four stops along the way. Our goal is to let everyone know about the Unseen Ruler, God, our Caring Creator. Then we are open to questions and after the difficult questions from the Mountain Youth, we are more ready for the question time of our meeting.

When we return, we rejoin Chihaysu and the other followers and will travel to the Valley People. This is the first time we will do this as a group. Chihaysu will give a speech on the shoreline. We hope that many, whom we have invited, will join us but do not know how everyone will respond. Jonas said we should call this the "Speech on the Shore."

Chihaysu advised that he will talk about God's promise: life after death. This is a mysterious idea to we, who live in Caperston. We think of death as the end and we strive to live our lives well to receive a special spot in the House of the Dead. The idea of life after death never occurred to me. I am interested in what Chihaysu will say.

Your friend,
Mattpaul

DATE . . . OCTOBER 28TH

Hi Alex and Tim,

I know no one has written, but I am too excited not to write. Chihaysu's Speech on the Shore was amazing. My sister Rachaeling, her friend Michaeling, and Huchfee were there as were at least thirty people who came from the Mountain Villages, including four Mountain Youth. They were people Marcus and I had just invited to join us.

Rachaeling told me that I now look much older and wiser since I joined Chihaysu. Michaeling looked so pretty. She has long, sandy red hair and the nicest smile. She said everyone looks up to me for what I have done. Even Huchfee said the same. Everyone seemed interested in what Chihaysu has to say.

Rachaeling is, like Dawnling, a year younger than the rest of us. She is especially close to our mother. She and Michaeling have been best friends since the first year of Lower School. Early on in her schooling my sister took to music. She could hear a song once and repeat the melody perfectly. Michaeling said that she has a musical ear. Rachaeling would sometimes join Michaeling when she went to Ms. Betty's house but, instead of reading, she would teach those in attendance a song. They loved the change from listening to stories to singing and these moments of helping brought my sister and Michaeling even closer together. I am not surprised that they came together to hear Chihaysu speak.

This, we all agreed, was the best speech Chihaysu has ever made. After the speech he asked if anyone would like to affirm their belief in God. Those who replied, "yes," were taken into the water behind the rock from which he spoke. He asked them if they wanted their wrongs forgiven and if they wanted the spirit of God to come to them. Then he slowly dropped them backwards into the water and, when he brought them out, they were clean of all wrong-doing. He called this act baptism.

I volunteered to do this, but Chihaysu said it was for everyone except his special followers. Many people came forward. Rachaeling wanted to but was afraid father would find out. Huchfee was not sure, but Michaeling did not hesitate. She was the third person in line for the washing. The fourth person was the man who talked to trees. He seemed different and thanked Michaeling for her effort to be kind to him, apologizing for not responding.

Chihaysu said so many things in his speech. I will try to remember some of them. He stated, "The poor, who believe, will be given the kingdom of God" and "Those who are humble will inherit the world." He gave us a warning: "Do not pray if you are angry with someone but settle your differences with that person first and then you are ready to pray." He told us to love our enemies and to pray for them. Our kindness may make them a friend. He said it is easy to love your friends but, with the help of God, loving our enemies will make this world a better place to live.

Then Chihaysu said something that really made me think. "Do not keep riches for yourself in Caperston. You will not keep them after you die." He said that maybe riches will get you a fancy tomb in the House of the Dead. But we believers will not be there. After we die, we will meet again with other believers in the mansion of God. When he said this there was complete silence in the crowd. No one in Caperston ever imagined that there was life after death. One young man, who I do not know, asked the question, "But we place our bodies in the House of the Dead. How can this be?"

Chihaysu replied, "We have bodies and we have souls. The House of the Dead is for our bodies, but the mansion of God is for our souls." Another person asked, "How will we know which soul belongs to a relative or friend?" Chihaysu replied that we all know those special things, which make us loved. These are spiritual characteristics not physical traits. These traits will be evident in the souls, living in the mansion God is preparing.

A schoolteacher of mine walked forward and asked, "Teacher, you have taught us many things. What is the most important thing you can teach us, the thing that truly makes our lives different?" Chihaysu responded by reminding him that there are two teachings.

The first is "Love God with all of your heart." The second is "Love all your neighbors as you love yourself." With that statement Chihaysu left and we followed him. No one said anything for some time, as we were all deep in thought.

As I left, I looked over my shoulder and I could see Rachaeling and Michaeling waving and smiling at me. I have never felt as happy as I did at that moment.

Mattpaul

DATE . . . OCTOBER 29TH

Mattpaul,

In the midst of my struggles, your optimism inspires me. I need an inoculation of hope.

Laura tells me she will not give up on me. She says that she prays every night that the pain I feel will go away. I am truly thankful for her prayers. However, if God somehow planned for Kevin's death, I just cannot accept this. I told Laura, perhaps too harshly, that I do not need her prayers. I need a miracle.

Alex

8

Challenges are Arising

DATE . . . OCTOBER 30TH

Alex, my friend,

Try to remember the good person Kevin was. As I have travelled with Chihaysu, I have heard him and others talk of Jonton. They remember him, his goodness, his courage, so favorably. Jonton is an inspiration for Chihaysu. He disappeared when he was in the middle of his second generation, leaving his wife and a young son. His son completed school three years ago and works for the man who builds houses in Caperston. He is learning this trade and one day hopes to take over the business. It is a good job as we only have one carpenter/builder in Caperston. Everyone needs help at some time during the year.

People remember Jonton whenever his son comes to their home to help out. They remember his father as someone who gave up his life because those in power did not like the fact that he stood up for the Mountain People. Even most Valley People remember him fondly.

Likewise, you and others will remember Kevin for his kindness.

Now I must tell you: challenges are arising in Caperston. When we left the Speech on the Shore, we walked for quite some time. Then a hunched over man approached us. He asked Chihaysu to assist him. Chihaysu replied, "How can I help?"

The man replied, "I hurt my back in a boating accident. Will you heal me?" Chihaysu replied, "I do not perform healings; only God can heal. You need to pray with all of your heart." The man then asked, "I do not know how to pray. What do I say?"

Chihaysu gave us an example of a prayer:

> *"Our God, who is caring and who loves us,*
> *Bring your loving ways to our world.*
> *May we do what you would have us do, as those who now live with you do.*
> *Help us with all of our challenges, the challenges of body and of soul*
> *for you are the true ruler of the world*
> *Let us never forget."*

The man thanked Chihaysu and walked away, struggling, but seemed encouraged. Later, before we went to sleep, I asked Chihaysu to repeat the prayer and I entered it into my compol.

That same night, as we were about to sleep, I looked across Lake Gael at the houses on the shoreline. It seemed strange that all, but one of the houses, were dark. We had seen this row of houses fully lit up most nights. I also noted something in the sky. There were five stars, all in a circular fashion, which I had seen many times before. But this time I noticed three more stars, in a straight line from the top of the circle down to the left and then beneath the circle of stars. It reminded me of Michaeling and her long, sandy red hair falling over her shoulders. I have never felt like this before. I am glad she smiled at me when I saw her waving.

The next day we reached the first village and Chihaysu was planning to speak. Present were Dawnling and her parents. Marcus and I greeted them. Dawnling stated that after Marcus and I left the meeting with the Mountain Youth, she felt an inner strength come over her. She returned to the youth, and said, "I am the one Chihaysu helped heal. I know God exists and I feel him in my heart." The Mountain Youth, realizing that she was one of their kind, came to her, hugged her and asked her to teach them to pray. Dawnling asked them to think about everything they had learned. Then she asked them to repeat the following prayer:

> "Dear God, help me to feel you in my heart.
> Teach me to love others, my friends and even my enemies.
> Thank you for all the new things we are learning."

The youth repeated the phrases she taught and promised to say them each morning in order to start the day with God and love for each other on their minds.

After speaking with Dawnling, but before Chihaysu spoke, Huchfee appeared. He had left his home as the sun came up and was here to warn us that problems were arising amongst the wealthy living in the lake houses. In addition, the Upper School teacher, who had asked the question about "the most important thing you can teach us," was going to speak tonight, challenging Chihaysu's teachings. Chihaysu listened and asked me to return with Huchfee and hear what this teacher was saying. If we left right away, we would make it in time for the speech.

Huchfee and I left and talked about many things. We talked about Michaeling and Huchfee said that she liked me. I admitted that I liked her. We talked about a new job Huchfee would be starting in a few days, working for my father. It will pay him much more money than he makes now, but it is not clear what his duties will be. He felt he had to take advantage of the opportunity.

We arrived at the house on the lake, which had the lights on the other night. It was a large house and almost one hundred people were present. To our surprise, my father was the first speaker. He approached with a classmate of mine, Zester, who stood next to father. We were surprised that father chose Zester as he was often in trouble at school and father had always claimed that he would only give jobs to good students.

Father thanked everyone for coming and stated that recent discoveries had been made that we all needed to hear. He introduced the teacher who spoke for a long time. I will try to summarize his two points. The first is that scientists had tested the genetics of the Valley People and the Mountain People and found that some Mountain People are genetically closer to certain animals than they are to the Valley People. When Chihaysu talks about equality, the teacher claims he is scientifically wrong. He used as an example the kickuml game. Only an inferior being would think of using his head to move a ball towards the goal of the opponent. Kickuml was meant to be a sport of the feet. He argued that hitting the ball with a person's head could cause injury. As he spoke, I remembered that by using their heads to move the ball forward, the Mountain Youth were more skilled than we were and won the match. I also remember getting guidance from Marcus as to this skill. When I tried it and did the skill correctly, my head felt fine. I appreciated Marcus coaching me.

Then the teacher stated that he had researched the origin of the House of the Dead. The first House of the Dead was built over 100 generations ago and was the creation of a man named Platos. Platos taught that citizens needed motivation to work for the common good. In hopes of earning a prominent place in the House of the Dead, one would work responsibly. In contrast, upon realizing that criminal actions would result in their bodies being thrown into the pit, people would be discouraged from harming others. The House of the Dead is an important building and, when Chihaysu talks about life after death in a mansion created by the unknown God, he disrespects it.

My father then spoke and stated that the Ruler, Pontos, has designated a holiday for three days from now. No one will work but everyone, who comes to visit the House of the Dead and leaves a memorial there, will be paid a full day's wage. Everyone cheered and many called for Chihaysu to be arrested so that he could not continue to teach his negative ideas. The meeting was over late in the evening and I went to Huchfee's home to rest. The next day I returned to Chihaysu.

Mattpaul

DATE . . . NOVEMBER 1ST

Dear Alex,

I write again because things are happening quickly.

Chihaysu was speaking to a large group. His message was a shortened version of his Speech on the Shore and we called it the Speech on the Mountain. When he was done, he saw a Mountain Youth named Dustin and his sister, Angeling, take sandwiches and break them into pieces to share with others in the crowd. Dustin later told me that Angeling made extra sandwiches to share with friends at the meeting but, to him, it did not matter who was hungry. Whether they knew the person coming to them or not, they shared their sandwiches until they ran out.

Chihaysu called them forward and told the crowd what they had done. Suddenly others came forward with food they had brought. Chihaysu broke the food into pieces and gave it to us to distribute. Many people also came forward to share their food.

It was a miracle of common sharing and, before we were done, everyone was fed. Chihaysu advised those attending to share like this every day of their lives.

It was a good example of how we should practice caring for not only our friends but all people in need.

Later that day he warned us that difficult times were coming, but he felt he had to go to the holiday at the House of the Dead. Three of us would come and the rest would remain behind to assist the Mountain People. I was one of those chosen to come.

Mattpaul

DATE . . . NOVEMBER 3RD

Jonas, Marcus and I went to the House of the Dead with Chihaysu. When we arrived, there were many people planning to enter. Chihaysu said we could enter, if we wished, but he had to go in alone.

When Chihaysu exited, there was a tear in his eye. Since he wanted to enter alone, we did not ask him what happened. He then saw a man selling memorials for people to take to the House of the Dead. They were small pictures of Pontos, the Ruler, with three lines at the bottom where a message could be written but only with a special pen. Chihaysu asked how much the memorials cost and was told 15 denorites, a reasonable amount. The seller then stated that we could only leave a message with a special pen. Chihaysu asked the cost of the pen and was told 100 denorites.

Chihaysu became angry and replied, "You give people a holiday to visit the House of the Dead then you charge more than a day's wage to leave a memorial! Whose idea was this?" The man stated that it was my father's idea. Chihaysu stated, "You tell Mattpaul's father it is a bad idea. It is only the body that resides in the House of the Dead. The living soul resides in the mansion of God." When those all around heard him say this, they complained, saying that he visited the House of the Dead and now says it is unimportant. We then left.

One young man seemed to be following us for some time after we left. Chihaysu stopped, turned around, and approached him. "What do you want, my friend?" The young man replied that he lived in one of the houses on the lake and wanted to follow Chihaysu. Chihaysu asked him why and the man said that he had heard the Speech on the Shore and had been thinking about it ever since. Once he heard what Chihaysu said to the man selling the memorials, he knew he wanted to be a follower.

Chihaysu advised him, "Go home and pick out a few necessary provisions, no more than a bag full. Then plan for a servant to open your house to the homeless in Caperston so they can escape living in the poor house. Give them three meals, not one, each day and have someone counsel them on how they can improve their lives. Then you can become my follower."

The man replied that he would pack a few belongings but was uncertain about opening his house to the poor. He explained that he feared heirlooms, left by his grandfather, would be taken. Chihaysu replied that, when we share our possessions with those in need, it was the same as sharing them with God himself. The man left us, looking sad. Chihaysu told us that it is exceedingly difficult for the rich to become followers of God. We all understood.

We planned to walk to the east side of Lake Gael where we would rest before continuing to the villages in the north. However, it has been raining on and off for two days and the rain is getting stronger. We will wait to leave, and I am happy to have time to write you this message.

Mattpaul

9

Arrested

DATE . . . NOVEMBER 4TH

Dear friends,

    The next morning, once the rain stopped, we began our journey to Lake Gael. However, several soldiers appeared and Chihaysu, Jonas and I were stopped. Marcus was allowed to continue on the journey to the north side of Lake Gael, while we three were taken to my father's home. Chihaysu and Jonas were then taken to a room in town across from the House of the Dead. A guard was assigned to assure that they did not leave. My sister Rachaeling came to me and I asked what was happening. Rachaeling explained that it was the rains that caused this. I asked, "What do you mean, Rachaeling?"

I must share this before continuing. We have rain in Caperston, but just enough to keep the plants flourishing. It rains once every seven to ten days. However, yesterday it began to rain extremely hard and only two days after the previous rain. The rain briefly stopped this morning but started up again in the afternoon. The houses near the lake were becoming flooded. The elders of Caperston report that it had not rained this hard for generations.

Rachaeling stated that the people, living on the lake, asked Pontos for help. They did not know what to do. The Mountain People also had rain, but their houses were built into the rocks of the mountains and their houses were not in danger. Pontos sent my father to speak for him. Father blamed the problem on Chihaysu, claiming Chihaysu practiced magic and the magic caused the rains and flooding.

Rachaeling said that mother wanted me to stay at home. She agreed with mother and tried to persuade me that, although Chihaysu was a good man, it was dangerous to be with him. She also told me her friend, Michaeling, was asking about me. "Michaeling likes you. You should stay." It is nice to know that Michaeling likes me. I was tempted to stay but let me tell you what happened next.

The rains started up much stronger and father had a scientist test a machine he was working on. It was a light machine. He could aim it at the clouds and a beam of light would go up to the sky. Father brought the

scientist, Chihaysu and Jonas outside. He told Chihaysu to try his magic
to stop the rain. If he could not, then the scientist would do so. Chihaysu
requested that the scientist go first. He stated that the scientist worked hard
on his light machine and should have the first opportunity. The scientist
aimed his machine upwards. We could see a beam of light hit the clouds. He
moved the beam of light back and forth and the rain slowed then stopped.
The clouds began to separate. Everyone cheered for the scientist. Chihaysu
congratulated him for his efforts.

But as soon as the rain stopped, the clouds began to again thicken and
this time they turned black. They started moving in a circular motion. Then
the rain came down harder than before. A large swirling cloud appeared
and started to come down towards the land. Everyone present cried out for
the scientist to aim his machine at it and he tried but was unsuccessful. The
wind knocked it up into the air and everyone ran for protection.

Only Chihaysu and Jonas remained. They knelt in front of the House
of the Dead and prayed. In a short time, the winds slowed. Then the rain
stopped; the clouds dispersed, and blue sky appeared. The storm was over.
The people congratulated Chihaysu and stated that they wanted him to remain and use his magic to protect them. Chihaysu replied that he did not
use magic and that he, himself, did nothing to stop the storm except to pray

and ask for God's help. He urged everyone to pray and told the story of Dawnling, of how her family had prayed and how she recovered. He and Jonas then left, and father did not dare to stop them.

I did not leave with them as Chihaysu had earlier told me that I must honor my father and my mother. He said that they deserve to clearly understand why I am choosing to follow him. I will try to talk to father one last time. At this moment he is pleased that I did not go with Chihaysu. Besides, I do want to see Michaeling, and Rachaeling said that she will invite her over today. I feel lucky that she is asking about me. I have never had a girlfriend. However, I have not given up my desire to follow Chihaysu. I will tell Michaeling and Rachaeling that I feel Chihaysu's message about the invisible God is important for everyone to hear.

Mattpaul

DATE . . . NOVEMBER 7TH

Dear Alex,

The contest between Chihaysu and the Scientist continues to be the talk of the town. Huchfee was asked by his editor to interview people about what they are now thinking after the contest. You remember that he got an award for his work with the daily newsletter.

For this occasion, he was not to take notes. This time he was asked to write a report for a special edition of "News of Yesterday, Today and Tomorrow." However, since the scientist was in no mood to give a weather forecast it became simply, "News of Yesterday and Today."

Huchfee received permission to take a day off from work and set up a table across from a food store, where people came to pick up groceries. He asked them three questions. Were they present when Chihaysu stopped the rainstorm by praying? If not, had they heard about this and from whom?

Lastly, who would they trust Chihaysu or the scientist if Caperston had to face a rainstorm like this again?

Huchfee received thirty seven replies before he had to leave at midday to write his story. Twenty nine were from Valley People and eight from Mountain People. Of the twenty nine Valley People, twenty four had been present. Three had heard about it from a neighbor and two stated that a friend of the scientist told them about it. Of the Mountain People, only one had seen the event but it was the talk of the Mountain Village.

The results were interesting. All of the Mountain People and twenty five of the Valley People stated that they would choose Chihaysu, if the rainstorms came again. Two others pointed out that the scientist did have some success and that, although Chihaysu was successful this time, they needed more evidence that this prayer activity actually works. Two others were simply uncertain, one stating that Chihaysu may have been lucky when he prayed, and the storm would have dispersed without him praying.

Huchfee then quoted two people, who shared more information with him.

The first person was Jonton Jr., who stated that Chihaysu reminded him of his father. He stated that his father disappeared when he was very young. He remembered his father speaking of another man, who also believed that the Mountain People and the Valley People were equals. His father had an important meeting and said goodbye to everyone but never returned. No one knows what happened.

While Jonton was speaking, an older man was listening. He then stepped forward and stated that he knew more. "I was the man, who was meeting with your father. We knew that there was support from some Valley People to treat the Mountain People more equally. We had to prove that there were more than a few of us who believed this.

We were planning to do just what you did today. We were going to interview Valley People and see if they would support combining the Mountain School and the Valley Schools so that all students would receive equal education. Back then the Lower Schools were similar, but the Upper Schools were much different.

In the Upper Schools Mountain students had only a half day of class, then worked a full afternoon at a work program. Most girls were trained in homemaking with an emphasis on sewing, while boys went out on Lake Gael with an adult and fished. They loved doing this but never got an opportunity to learn the more varied topics which were available for Valley Students.

The day you remember last seeing your father was the day we were to take the survey. I went to the marketplace, but your father never appeared. I waited several hours then came to your home. Your mother told me that she only knew he had an important meeting that day. She gave me permission to speak with the police. When I went to their office, they were uninterested. 'Take a walk around Lake Gael. You will probably find him there. He was a troublemaker, you know.' I became afraid to continue our plan so that was the end of it.

I am getting old, but I am enthused to hear Chihaysu speak out. It has been a long time that the Mountain People have been treated unfairly."

The next day the newsletter only had one piece of news. It was Huchfees article and people were very impressed.

Mattpaul

10

The Chest of Visions

Mattpaul, my friend,

It has been three weeks since I have heard from you. Are you there? Are you safe? Did your compol break down? I feel alone without your letters. Please write.

Alex

DATE . . . DECEMBER 10TH

Dear Alex and Tim,

I know you must be wondering what has happened. I see the last letter was written some time ago. Let me tell you. My name is Huchfee. I know Mattpaul has spoken of me. Yes, I am the person who took the survey and wrote the article about the scientist and Chihaysu for the daily newsletter.

Mattpaul will no longer be writing.

Two nights after the contest between the scientist and Chihaysu, Mattapaul's father was angry. He was not the only one. Yes, as you know from my survey, most Valley People were happy that Chihaysu's prayer stopped the storm. However, there were some, particularly those who lived in the lake houses, who were not. After reading my article in the "News of Yesterday and Today," they went with Mattpaul's father the next morning to ask Pontus to arrest Chihaysu and put him on trial. That same morning Mattpaul left to rejoin Chihaysu and his followers.

That evening several soldiers were sent to the place where Chihaysu and his followers were resting. When they arrived Chihaysu had walked away to pray. The soldiers called out, "Which one of you is Chihaysu?" No one responded. Then a young soldier pointed to Mattpaul and said, "That is him, the troublemaker." The soldiers arrested Mattpaul.

When they returned, his father realized the mistake but sent Mattpaul to prison. It was a dark, dry place. The orders were to give him no food until he admitted that he was wrong to be a follower of Chihaysu and that Chihaysu was a fraud. His father had decided that this was a better tactic than actually arresting Chihaysu. He did not understand how strong and courageous his son had become.

For three days Mattpaul was imprisoned in the dark, dry place with no nourishment. He became weaker but whenever he was asked to denounce Chihaysu, he refused.

I had just begun working for Mattpaul's father and one day, when I was about to leave work, I was taken to see my oldest friend. It was the fourth night after his arrest. He was very weak and hot to my touch. He could only speak softly a word or two at a time. Mattpaul whispered (that is all he could do) "my belt." I looked along his belt and a small key was attached on a string to it. He said, "Take it to Rachaeling."

He had two guards overseeing him. When I felt his forehead, it was burning. I asked, "Can you give me water for him to drink and something to cool his forehead." One guard, Zester, stated that Mattpaul was a traitor and he was better off dead. The other guard said nothing. A short time later Zester excused himself, leaving briefly, and the second guard stepped away, returning with a wet, cool cloth. "Here, wet his head and comfort him," he said. I did so and Mattpaul fell into a deep sleep, his head on my lap. I too fell asleep and, when I awoke the next morning, my dearest friend was dead.

I reported this to Zester, who had denied Mattpaul water the previous day. Zester stated that he would take care of the matter. He escorted me out of the prison and told me that I should go home.

Later that evening, I was summoned to see his father. His father asked me what happened, and I explained. He became upset that no one alerted him to Mattpaul's condition. He swore his intention was not to kill him but to leave him alone, without food, to motivate him to think through decisions he had made.

He asked if Mattpaul had discussed his faith and all I could say was that he was too weak to talk. His father asked, "Who denied him water?" I told him the story of the kind guard who brought me the wet towel for Mattpaul's head, but his father said this one act of kindness was not enough. "The guards will be fired," he announced, "They should have advised me of Mattpaul's deteriorating condition." I asked about Mattpaul's mother and sister, Rachaeling. He stated that they are grieving together and wish to be alone. He respects their wishes. He then thanked me stating, "You were a true friend of my son."

I came to work the next day and was given a variety of tasks, none of which involved Mattpaul or Chihaysu. No one said anything about plans for Mattpaul's body. Would there be a place in the House of the Dead for him? I did not know.

When I arrived the following day, I was brought to a mobile. This is a vehicle in which six individuals can sit. It travels faster than the fastest runner in Caperston. Only the rich and powerful have one. Most of us do not need a mobile as we walk from our homes to job sites, stores and meeting places. When I approached the mobile, I saw Rachaeling and Michaeling in the back seat. The driver turned it on and took us on a long journey. When he stopped he pointed to a path. We got out and followed it. At the end of the path was an area in the ground that had recently been dug up and refilled and a stone marker was placed on top of it. Nothing was written on the marker.

Michaeling reached into a bag she had brought and took out a wooden plaque. Burned into it was the following message:

Mattpaul

> *God and all those in the mansion of God*
> *know how faithful you have been*
> *and how you have brought light*
> *into our world*

Michaeling left the plaque on top of the marker. As we walked back to the mobile, we saw a second marker off to the right. It was covered with mud. I brushed it off and saw it had simply one word: *Jonton*. When we returned home, I told Rachaeling of the key latched to Mattpaul's belt. She took it and said, "See me after your workday is over at the marketplace."

Later Rachaeling met me. She said that the key was to a safe in her home. She and Mattpaul each had their own safe. She went to his safe and found many papers, copies of letters Mattpaul had sent to you. She read the letters that afternoon and told me I had to read them then share them with Chihaysu. Rachaeling said that she made a copy of all the letters for herself.

Two days later was my day off. I walked to the northeast side of Lake Gael where Chihaysu was staying, just a little south of the villages. He met me and asked if I knew anything of Mattpaul. I told him the events of the past days. Chihaysu said that when Mattpaul was taken, he assumed it would be, as in the past, a day or two of interrogation and then a release. He insisted that, if he had suspected the possibility of what happened, he would have gone to the authorities and offered himself in Mattpaul's place. Then he cried deeply and for some time.

I showed him the letters you and Mattpaul were sharing. After he read the first three, he put them down. Chihaysu said, "I need to tell you who I am." He then told his story.

He started, "You remember when I went to the House of the Dead a while ago? I was going to pay tribute to my father." He continued, "My father was a Valley Person who lived on the shore of the lake. He worked for the Ruler and was asked to visit the Mountain People and report where they lived, how many communities there were and if the communities worked together. This was a short time before the census you have learned about in school.

He spent twenty days traveling and talking to the Mountain People. During his travels he met a beautiful Mountain Girl. She was kind to him and, after he finished his work, he asked if he could visit her. To make a long story short, they fell in love. My father brought her to meet his family. When they realized she was a Mountain Girl, though they were courteous to her, they privately told my father that he had to choose between them and the Mountain Girl. He could not marry her and bring her home to live in the Valley community. My father was distressed but chose the girl, who was my mother. He quit his job and moved in with the Mountain People.

He learned to be a fisherman. When my mother was about to give birth to me, there was a census and my parents had to meet with a registrar. It was then that the authorities learned that father had married a Mountain Girl. My parents returned and shortly afterwards I was born. My mother said the days after my birth were the happiest days of her life. "I had my two men, your father and yourself," she told me. Unfortunately, this was only for a short time. One night there was a knock on the door and two soldiers appeared. They took my father with them, and my mother never saw him again.

I was raised by my mother and knew nothing of my father until I was half a generation old. Then my mother told me his story and about the House of the Dead. She had never visited it but wondered if it might give an accounting of what happened to my father.

Sometime later I visited the House of the Dead. I found my father's tomb. It was one of the nicer ones, but off to the far side of the building. There was a notation on a stone tablet to the right of his coffin. It described his exploration of the Mountain People that led to the census, but no mention of my mother or me. This was strange. All the other tombs, similar to the grave of my father, mentioned the father, mother, wife/husband and children of the deceased. Father's grave listed only his parents. I also looked at the book where visitors record their visits. Father's grave had one visitor, his mother. She had visited twelve times. His father never signed the book.

I signed the book and identified myself as his son, telling mother of my visit. She cried for her husband and for me because I never knew him.

A strange thing happened a few days later. A man came to our house with a small chest for me. I opened it and in it was a compol. I had never had one. There was an instruction book and inside the book was a note from my father's mother, my grandmother. It stated that she had waited, hoping that I would visit father's tomb in the House of the Dead. She now knew who I was, and she wanted to give me a gift. She stated that in the back of the instruction book was a second, special note. It was from my father. I immediately opened it.

The letter stated that he was sorry that he would not be there for me as the authorities had imprisoned him. While in prison they gave him duties. One was a research project. While completing the project, he discovered teachings by a man named Jesus. He found the teachings of great interest, particularly the teachings about prayer. He tried praying and, one day while praying, he felt a power take over him. He then had a series of three visions. They began in the afternoon when he could see the sunlight through his cell window. When they ended, he noticed it was dark outside.

The first vision was of me, his son, when I become a man. He wrote that he saw me speaking in front of small groups of the populace of Caperston, telling them of the being God. My listeners, in his vision, were attentive and responded enthusiastically.

The second vision was more troubling. He saw me being arrested and then put on trial. He wrote that he never saw the outcome of the trial but, rather, found himself peacefully floating above the mountains.

The last vision came shortly afterwards. He was taken from the mountain scenery to the government halls where he saw Mountain People and Valley People working together. He saw me in their midst and, after a few moments, awoke to the darkness of his cell.

My father left me a code and said I should put it into the compol, which I did. It brought me to another world called Earth and to a story, written by a man named Matthew, about this man Jesus. It also brought me to some teachings of a man named Paul and a third man named John. All the teachings were about this man Jesus. I read them over and over again. I became convinced that these teachings would bring the Valley and Mountain People together in equality.

When I was grown, I told my mother that I wanted to tell others of the teachings of this man Jesus and so I did. I began to gather special followers and I knew just by Mattpaul's name that God sent him to me. The others are trustworthy, but Mattpaul was special. I believe that it is young people like Mattpaul, Marcus and yourself who will bring about change in Caperston.

I studied what happened to the man Jesus, who they say was the son of God. He was killed by the leaders of his world. The writer Paul said Jesus had to die to make up for the wrongdoings of the people. I was not sure I would be strong enough to do as Jesus did and I determined to be careful in situations that would leave my life in jeopardy. I am just a man not the son of God. Your friend, Mattpaul, was a special young man. He had greater courage than I. Perhaps someone must die for the wrongdoings of the people of Caperston as Jesus died for the wrongdoings of the people of earth. I am not sure.

Every night I pray that this Jesus will someday visit us as he visited the inhabitants of Earth. I do not know if this is possible, but I will continue to ask God if it can be. I do not know what the future will hold. I do know this. On the place called Earth, Jesus said that the future would bring difficult times before God would intervene. I fear the same will be true for Caperston. Those in power want to continue the old ways of inequality, and we feel that inequality is not God's way. We will need strength in the future. Mattpaul's courage is giving me the strength to persevere."

When he finished, I was speechless. I left Chihaysu with all the letters and he promised to read them. I then returned to the Valley Community on the south shore of Lake Gael.

Later I met with Rachaeling and Michaeling. We walked to the rock by the shore where Chihaysu had once preached. It was the place Michaeling last saw Mattpaul and waved goodbye to him. I told them Chihaysu's story. We quietly sat there as the sun set. I felt content to be with my friends. Then Rachaeling leaned over and put her head on my shoulder. I felt so happy. The sky was now dark and Michaeling pointed to a circle of stars above. "Look Rachaeling," she said, "there are five stars in a circle and the three stars in a line from the top of the circle down the left side. It looks like you with your beautiful long, brown hair hanging over your shoulders."

Rachaeling smiled as she glanced at me. "Thank you, Michaeling," she replied. We both remembered when Mattpaul wrote how the same stars made him think of Michaeling. Someday I will tell Michaeling that, when she looks at these stars, she is looking at herself. But not tonight.

Huchfee

11

Heaven

Dear Huchfee,

Thank you for sharing Mattpaul's story. When I read of Mattpaul's death, I was angry. I was in my room and I called out to God, "Why? Why did you let Mattpaul die? He was as faithful to you as Kevin was and you let them both die. You are just an uncaring, useless being. Why take their lives? Why not take mine instead?"

Suddenly my anger went away. I became sleepy and lay down. That night I dreamed. I was in a small room and heard a knock on the door. When I opened it, a young man greeted me, "Hi," he said, "my name is Mattpaul; it is good to finally meet you."

He took me outside and pointed to a city a short distance away. It was beautiful. All the buildings were white, perhaps four or five floors high. Each building had a unique design upon it. "Oh, you see the sculptures on the roofs," Mattpaul said, "They are there so that, from a distance, we can all see which building is ours. Mine is the one on the left with the three angels playing horns." Around the city was a wall perhaps two stories high. It sparkled in a light brown color, contrasting just a bit with the white of the houses. There were inscriptions on the wall but from a distance. I could not read them. There appeared to be several gates in the wall to enter the city. Each gate had a unique arch upon it. Entering one gate, on the right, was a river, which exited through a second gate on the left. Around the river was a line of trees similar to palm trees with a bundle of large, white flowers on the top.

I turned to see the door that we had exited, and the room and its door were gone. We were standing in a garden of small evergreen trees. Interspersed amidst the trees was a ground cover of four-leaf clovers with small white flowers and beautiful gold centers, star like in shape. There was a path through the garden and, at the end of the path, an open field to which it led. Mattpaul stated that there would be two more evening visits and that this night's visit would be short. When I woke up, I should immediately write down what I saw so I would be accurate. I did so and it is what you are now reading.

I slept soundly after writing my account of the dream and wondered if the next night would bring a new dream. Just as promised Mattpaul appeared, but this time it was not in a room or the garden. We were standing in front of one of the gates to the city. I looked up and could see that on the walls there were lists of names of unknown beings.

We entered the city and passed down a road by several four and five story homes, modest in style, but the purest white I have ever seen. At the end of the street we came to a courtyard which seemed to be in the center of the city. In the middle of the courtyard was a stage and on the stage was a scaffold holding a tall purple curtain with a gold topping. As we walked closer to the center of the courtyard, I realized that I was standing in one of several courtyards surrounding the stage. A large crowd was gathering.

Mattpaul stated that he had to leave me as he walked to the stage and disappeared behind the curtain. Then I heard a chime and a short time later a much louder chime. The crowd became quiet and the purple and gold curtain opened. A woman dressed in white appeared and stated, "This is a special day, honoring two new residents. God has sent His son Jesus to honor them." A man, also dressed in white, appeared. I could not believe it. Was this truly Jesus?

The man stepped alongside of the woman and stated, "You have all been faithful. You are people with not simply head knowledge of the things of faith but heart knowledge. You have helped all your fellow beings from each of your worlds. Today we recognize that some people are not only filled with heart knowledge, but also made the ultimate sacrifice. They were lights to their worlds, even though their lives were cut terribly short. They made a difference. Today their names will be listed on the city walls with all of the other martyrs who gave their life for their beliefs."

"Today I present to you, from the world called Caperston, Mattpaul, who died in prison because he refused to compromise his faith. I also bring to you from the world of Earth, Kevin, who died while feeding the hungry and the homeless." Jesus reached out both of his hands to his sides and Mattpaul appeared from the right and Kevin from the left. I began to sob, and my knees buckled. Two of those around reached down to pick me up. I could feel their supporting arms. Jesus stated, "People of God welcome these heroes to our home."

I then heard the inhabitants of heaven call out, in unison, "Praise be to God the Almighty and to His son Jesus and thank you for the lives of Mattpaul and Kevin." They repeated the saying three times and then I woke up.

There was one more day to pass and one more night to come. I fell asleep the next evening and was not disappointed. I dreamed I was in the garden of the first dream, looking out upon the beautiful city. I began to walk through the garden to the field and, when I reached it, a ball bounced past me from right to left. I turned to see its destination and saw Kevin kick the ball back to the right . . . to Mattpaul.

Kevin approached me. "Yes, we play soccer here, but guess what it is called?"

"What?" I replied, as I had no idea.

"Well, they call the game 'Kickuml' as it is called in Caperston," Kevin advised.

"Same rules" said Mattpaul, "except here we do not keep score. That way no one has an idea as to who is winning the game."

"And," Kevin concluded, "Everyone is a winner." He then continued, "When Mattpaul came here, I learned he had been corresponding with you, so I introduced myself and now we are best friends."

Then Mattpaul interjected, "We know it has been difficult for you to understand why things happened as they did. God did not predestine anything. However, he did know that a problem would occur. Although I have been able to contact you in dreams, I have been unable to contact Huchfee, Michaeling and the others though I have tried. So, I need you to send them a message. Will you do so, Alex?"

I replied that I certainly would. Mattpaul responded, "It is actually two messages. The first is that Chihaysu needs three followers, not one, to replace me so that he will now have twelve followers. At least one of those joining him should be female. The second message is this: chaos is coming to Caperston and there will be a new follower of Chihaysu that no one would expect." I asked who and he replied that he does not know the identity of the person, but that I should pass both messages along. I agreed to do so.

Kevin also made a request. He wants me to return to our old youth group and tell them of my dreams. But before speaking to them, I must speak to Laura. Kevin stated, "Laura prays every day that the pain you are experiencing will go away." With this request from Kevin received, I awoke.

Excuse me for not immediately sending these messages to you. I needed to see what the following days would bring. I will summarize. Three more nights have passed and there were no more dreams.

Two days after the third dream I spoke with Laura. There is a park down the block from our high school, and we walked there to a garden that resembled the one I recalled from my dream. We sat on a bench and I told her the whole story including my willingness to return to church and tell the youth members what I had experienced. Laura began to cry, saying, "You have come back to us, Alex . . . I am so happy."

I replied, "I didn't come back to you on my own; God brought me back."

In two days, I will return to church and share this story. The outcome of that meeting will be a part of my next correspondence. I wait to hear more about the coming events in Caperston. Which of you will replace Mattpaul as a follower of Chihaysu? Be assured that your friend, Mattpaul, is watching over you as our friend, Kevin, is looking down on the faithful of our world.

Alex

Appendix 1

The Science behind the Story

In the beginning there was God . . . so reads Genesis chapter one.

In the beginning there was a singularity. So states the most modern theories of cosmology, the study of the origin of the universe. This singularity was infinitely small, made up of the most elemental of atomic particles. These particles were in such constant movement that their location could never be identified. In a sense they were nowhere and yet everywhere.

Then at some moment about 14 billion years ago a gravity-defying force appeared and that singularity blew up in what has become known as the Big Bang. The universe expanded, cooled, and the element Hydrogen emerged, some of which became Helium. Eventually Carbon and Nitrogen were created and later, in the centers of stars, Iron and other higher elements appeared. Along with the creation of the elements came the laws of physics that explained how everything interacts. And so, Earth became Earth. Plants and animals appeared and then, humans. It seems simple in a way. But is it?

There are problems with this explanation. The laws that explain how the sun, planets, moons and stars interact are different than the laws that explain how atoms, quarks and elements of the quantum system (the building blocks of matter) operate. Can nature be governed by such divergent sets of laws?

Scientists struggled with this dichotomy of laws until string theory appeared. Strings are oscillating bits of energy, which make up all matter, all energy, everything. The smallest observable item contains billions of strings.

How small are they? If an atom were the size of the solar system with the nucleus being the sun and the planets being electrons circling the sun, a string would be the size of an average tree.

However, one of string theory's most dramatic predictions is that there are cosmic strings, which would be billions of light years long, thinner than a proton and spectacularly dense. So, a simple explanation of how Mattpaul could communicate with Earth is that his messages could be sent exceedingly long distances over these cosmic strings. Seems like a simple explanation except . . . Mattpaul lives in a parallel universe.

Fortunately, string theory offers a second explanation of how Mattpaul could communicate with Earth. Strings are active. They never remain in the same location and this is what is important to our story of Caperston and the ability of Mattpaul to communicate. Let me try to explain.

Strings move about so quickly that their whereabouts is unknown. Even strings billions of light years long are constantly in motion. Due to this movement it is difficult to predict the location of a string at any given time. We can surmise that a string exists in a certain area, but there exists a probability that it can be elsewhere. That elsewhere can be in a different, parallel universe.

Strings mold themselves into a structure called a Calibu-Yau. Information can enter into such a structure and theoretically pass through borders into different dimensions and/or different universes. This occurs because Calibu-Yau converts pieces of information into an electromagnetic stream of message bearing photons. Information is received and the Calibu-Yau explodes, disintegrating the photon stream then, instantaneously, recreates itself in another location, perhaps a location in a parallel universe.

With the stream recreating itself at a target, in this case a website, it is easy to comprehend how Mattpaul can send his messages. But how does he receive messages? According to the model, the energy stream has a return flow. This is common in nature. An example would be a magnetic field which bends back upon itself. Mattpaul's photon stream travels to the website then instantaneously returns to his compol with data to read.

But what of the messages sent from Earth to Caperston? We do not possess the capability of sending a message across the universal barrier. How does this occur? Simply speaking, it does not. You will note that at no time do Alex or Tim actually send a message to Mattpaul. Rather their reply to Mattpaul is entered onto a webpage for anyone to read. When Mattpaul communicates, he links to the website and reads the author's reply. If he chooses to reply, he must reenter the numerical sequence as his communication is a one moment, instantaneous event.

So, our story integrates individuals from two parallel universes and, because the universes are parallel in nature, the informational flow is instantaneous. If Mattpaul were to live in a distant solar system, the correspondence would not be possible as the distance the photon stream would have to travel would be much too long. Even a planet around the nearest star to our solar system would require eight years for a message sent to receive a response.

Mattpaul reported, in an unpublished correspondence, that he entered his address and a personal identification number he had received, as a resident of Caperston, into his compol. It was these digits, which led to his contact with the website on Earth. Is it simply fortuitous that Mattpaul's personal numbers just happened to correspond to the website identity? Or was there more to it than simply good fortune? Was this simply a chance occurrence? Or was there some other influential factor?

In the beginning there were strings, wrapped together in an infinitely small singularity. In the end, there was the Alpha and the Omega, the beginning and the ending. There was God.

Appendix 2

Not Just a Story: A Lesson in Life

YOUTH GROUP STUDY

Three approaches are suggested to study this story.

Approach #1:

The dates of Mattpaul's letters begin in late April and end during the following December covering a span of eight months. Take time each meeting to read and discuss the letters received in corresponding dates since the last meeting. Thus, if you begin the study in September, you will end in April or May. Ask youth to place himself or herself in the role of Mattpaul. How would they react if Chihaysu came to earth and they were being challenged to follow him?

Prepare youth before reading the first letter by asking them to imagine that Jesus had never come to earth. How would the world be different today? Would God have sent other prophets over the last 2,000 years? After discussing, ask them, for the purpose of this study, to imagine that Jesus had not come but that God's message and his promise had been shared by a continuum of prophets.

Approach #2:

Focus on the responses of Alex to the events happening in Caperston and of his growing friendship with Mattpaul. Look at his internal conflict. Why did God allow his best friend and committed Christian youth, Kevin, die? Discuss how the story Mattpaul shares helps Alex.

Then ask youth to identify their own moments of doubt, particularly in regard to faith and to acting upon it. Focus on what Mattpaul does when he wonders about all the new ideas he is learning. Discuss the concept that a working definition of faith is:

"Faith is saying 'yes' to the Word of God."

Point out that we Christians receive instruction by reading the Bible and acting accordingly. In Caperston Mattpaul, Rachaeling, Michaeling, Marcus and the other youth learn of God's will through direct contact with Chihaysu.

Approach #3:

Talk about the opportunities of youth in Caperston and youth on earth. Alex talks about wishing he could be in the presence of Chihaysu to speak to him face-to-face. Mattpaul speaks of wishing he had parents who would support his faith journey as Alex's parents support him, even to the degree of letting him leave the church until he is ready to return.

Only when you have finished the story ask the youth the following: which would they prefer: the world of Caperston, where they can see and speak face-to-face with the prophet Chihaysu, or the world of earth, where we cannot speak to Jesus face-to-face but where we have the actual words of God's son recorded for us to study?

INDIVIDUAL LESSONS:

After choosing an approach review the below lessons and pick those that would be of most interest to your youth.

Lesson One:

Read the letter of May 8th. Compare the story that Chihaysu tells about the man in the water needing help with the Good Samaritan story of Jesus found in Luke 19: 25–37. How are they similar? In what ways are they different? Is there any justification given for those who made excuses not to help? If you were in the Caperston story, riding in a safe boat and came upon this man what would you do? Would you empty the boat of the fish it took a day for you to catch in order to rescue this man?

When have the students had the challenge of being confronted by someone in need? We all know that bullying, especially among teenagers, is a problem. Ask them: "What would you do if you see a fellow student picked on, whether it is a physical and/or a verbal act? Would you walk away, saying to yourself, that's not my problem, someone else will take care of it?" If this is the response, are the youth not like the two men who saw the man in the water and drove their boats away? What is the correct response to the child being picked on and to the person doing the bullying?

Lesson Two:

Read the letter of May 26th. Is this a miracle? Read the Biblical story in Luke 8: 49–56 that is similar. The Biblical story is considered a miracle because Jesus says, "Get up child." and "her life returned." In the Caperston story Chihaysu prays with the parents for the healing of Dawnling and she is healed. Is this also a miracle? If so, are there modern day miracles when prayer is made to God and healing occurs, even though medical science suggests recovery is not possible?

Review Mattpaul's reaction to prayer found in the letters dated May 2nd and August 23rd. How comfortable is each youth with prayer? Below is an activity that can be used to help youth understand the power and the comfort of prayer.

Trust and Prayer

Begin by presenting the following scenario. You have come to youth group and are facing a difficult situation and need someone to talk whom you can trust. Ask youth to raise their hand if there is one person in youth group (not counting adults) whom they feel comfortable talking to. They do not have to identify the person.

Then ask how many have two, three or four friends they can truly trust. Take time to discuss what makes a person trustworthy. In our group the following were the most common characteristics mentioned: being a good listener, not being judgmental and having had a positive trusting experience in the past.

Read Proverbs 3:5. Discuss how difficult it is to trust in the Lord with all your heart and not to depend on your own understanding of things.

Now take time to ask youth to share one thing that they would like to see changed. The change reported may be about themselves, the youth group, their families, their school or the world. Point out that sharing such important things requires a trust in each other. As youth share their thoughts, take time to briefly discuss the requests made then write them down on a piece of paper large enough for all to see.

Ask youth to sit "Indian style" in a circle. Have some small candles available that can be held, one for each youth. Read the requests for change that have been recorded. Now advise youth that we will pray for these as follows. A youth leader will light a candle and pray referencing at least several of the recorded requests for change. Once the leader has completed his or her prayer, youth are invited to light their own candle and verbally pray for all to hear. The list of things to be changed is made available for those who need it. After a couple of candles have been lit, extinguish the lights in the room.

When we did this event, one of our youth asked, "Do you mean pray out loud?" and I replied "Yes, that is what trust is all about." Though only an eighth grader, he was willing to participate. When all youth, who wish to participate, have prayed, the youth leader should say a concluding prayer and then ask youth to see how their candles have brightened the room. Advise that our prayers bring light and hope to people. Extinguish the candles one by one noting the contribution each youth's candle made to overcome the darkness of the room. Focus on the light left from the one candle, how it can brighten the room.

Advise that one youth saying one prayer to God is as all-encompassing as the one lit candle is able to light up the entire room.

Lesson Three:

Review the July 7th and the July 25th letters which discuss the man who talks to trees. He is interested in what Chihaysu teaches but does not want to communicate with others including Huchfee, Mattpaul and Michaeling. He climbs a tree so he can hear Chihaysu and yet not have to interact with others.

Yet he gives a clue that he is opening up to others. On July 25th he responds, when approached by Mattpaul and the others, "Not today, not today" then is observed taking notes as Chihaysu speaks. We next meet him when he is baptized on October 28th. At that time he thanks Michaeling for her efforts to be kind to him.

First ask youth to identify what might be causing the man, who talks to trees, to be so afraid to decline to respond to the kindness of the young people. Ask the youth if they know anyone, perhaps someone at school, who is likewise fearful of interactions. Then read Matthew 25: 31–40 and discuss if reaching out to the man who talks to trees is an example of what Jesus was calling us to do. Ask youth to describe any times they have reached out to others. If they have problems coming up with past instances, perhaps a discussion about working in a local soup kitchen or reaching out to an elderly person in the congregation/community can follow. The bullying discussion referenced in Lesson One would also apply in this discussion.

Lesson Four:

Note that on July 25th Dawnling states, "This is what faith is: saying 'yes' to the Word of God." She then states that she "hopes to hear something that I can do for others as God has helped me."

Then review the story of the goaderd from the August 12th letter. This goaderd truly made an extra effort to find the lost goada. He spent not one night but two nights looking, even after friends told him to forget about the lost animal.

Lastly review Alex's response to Mattpaul's October 28th letter. Alex writes, "Your optimism for the future of Caperston gives me hope. I need an inoculation of hope."

Paul writes in I Corinthians 13 of the three cornerstones of Christian belief: "faith, hope and love." Discuss how each of these three is depicted in the above scenes from the story. Dawnling talks about her desire to put faith into action. Think of her definition of faith: faith is "saying yes" to the word of God. Once we say "yes," action will follow.

The story of the goaderd and the missing goada is a story of the love the goaderd had for his missing animal and is a demonstration of the love God has for us. Discuss how many times youth have made this extra effort for a friend. Ask them to share examples.

Then point out how stories as these give "inoculations of hope" for those in need of hope. The event, which makes the difference for someone in need, is not a sermon but an action of love that spawns hope.

Lesson Five

Read the October 14th letter when Marcus and Mattpaul speak to the Mountain Youth. Share why some of the Mountain Youth are skeptical of the message of a caring God. Read their questions, "You talk about this man named God. Why does he send you? Can he not come and speak to us himself? Where does he live?" Ask youth if these are reasonable questions.

Then share the advice Chihaysu gives to Mattpaul: "God lives in the heart of those who believe in him" and Mattpaul's conclusion: "God is the light that shines out of me when I pray. God is light; he is the entity that brings brightness to the world."

This is an opportunity to discuss whether youth have experienced this type closeness to God. Do they feel his presence? Is there someone they know that brings brightness to the world? Perhaps the Trust and Prayer activity, which is described in Lesson Two, can be used in this lesson. Point out how much brightness just one candle, one prayer, brings to a darkened room.

Lesson Six:

In the letter of October 28th Chihaysu gives, what Jonas calls, his Speech on the Shore. Compare this speech to Jesus' Sermon on the Mount, recorded in Matthew chapters five through seven. How are they similar and how are they different? Remember that Caperston and Earth are in parallel universes so similarities will exist between individuals and, therefore, the way events play out respectively in the two worlds.

As an exercise, as youth read the remainder of the story, ask them to identify other teachings of the Sermon on the Mount, which are presented by Chihaysu elsewhere in the story?

Lesson Seven:

At the beginning of Chapter five, as recorded in the letter of August 25th, Chihaysu, while walking with his followers, stops and picks up a flower. He says, "Look at this flower. How beautiful it is. Every morning when the sun comes up, it reopens to show us the orange and red within. Then at night, it closes up to rest. God, our unseen ruler, created this flower and cares for it. It is why I call God our Caring Creator. If he can care for a flower like this so carefully that he makes sure it gets its rest each night, will he not care for every one of us. Remember this flower when your worries trouble you. We have a Caring Creator."

This statement by Chihaysu is similar to a statement by Jesus in Matthew 6:25–34. What are the similarities and the differences between the teachings of Chihaysu and of Jesus?

Then discuss Chihaysu's definition of God as a Caring Creator. Is this definition consistent with the teachings of Jesus?

Lesson Eight:

In the letter of December 10th, Chihaysu is telling the story of his father and of visions he had while in prison. Ask youth if they believe people can have visions. What type visions? Can individuals have visions about the future and, if so, what does that suggest about the future? Does it suggest that the future has already been determined? This is a theme in the death of Kevin that is discussed at various segments of the book. It is also discussed in the dream Alex has of Kevin and Mattpaul in heaven.

What are the differences between the dream of Alex and the vision of Chihaysu's father? What are their similarities?

Read Joel 2:28 and advise youth that this passage was so meaningful to the Apostle Peter that he quotes it in his Pentecost speech recorded in Acts chapter two. What does Joel mean when he says, "Your old men will have dreams and your young men will see visions"?

More discussion and activities on the topic of Dreams and Visions can be found in Chapter 10 of the book, "Not the Same Old, Done-it-before Youth Meetings" also authored by Tim Ferguson.

Lesson Nine:

Take time to describe each of the youth in the story. Make a copy of the picture of the young people with Chihaysu, found at the beginning of the book, and display it for all to see. Ask youth to describe each youth in the story, first one youth from the Valley Group on the left then one of the Mountain Group on the right. Make a chart with categories as follows:

Name	Valley or Mountain	Most Important Action Taken	One Word Description
Mattpaul	Valley	Did not deny his faith even in prison	brave
Dawnling	Mountain	Determined to put faith into action	caring

By "one word description" adjectives like timid, brave, unsure, caring, funny, committed, intimidated and the like might be used.

Then ask the youth to identify which of the youth they are most like at present and which they would like to emulate. This may be the same person or someone different. For example, someone might describe themselves as timid, which might describe Rachaeling, but they would like to be committed as Michaeling demonstrated she was when she was the third person in line to be baptized.

Lesson Ten:

Reread the letter of September 22nd. Jonas, his friend Levee, and Mattpaul climb into Levee's boat for a ride across Lake Gael. The weather was nice when they left but partway across the lake a storm arrives, and the boat is tossed about. Levi struggles to regain control of the boat and the men are fearful that it will overturn. Mattpaul calls out, "God help us." Chihaysu hears this and waves his hand and the storm passes.

Read Mark 4:36–41. Compare this story to the story of Jonas, Levi and Mattpaul. In Mark's story Jesus is sleeping while the storm is threatening them. His disciples call out to Jesus, "Teacher, don't you care that we are about to die?" Jesus responds to them "Why are you frightened? Do you still have no faith?"

One interesting difference is that Mattpaul calls out directly to God, not to Chihaysu on the shore. He is a new disciple but has enough faith to petition God himself. Jesus' response to his disciples is: "do you still have no faith?" Does the youth Mattpaul have a greater faith than the seasoned disciples of Jesus? Are youth more likely to believe than adults?

Continue reading this story and the following passage arises:

We have a large tree in Caperston and Chihaysu took a seed that fell from it. He said, "See how small the seed is and now look at the great tree that has grown from it. Your faith will grow to be large like this tree." He taught us that, in this way, we are similar to the tree but, in other ways, we are much different. The tree has no consciousness. It does not think. But God made something great out of something so little. What can he do with each of us if we truly believe and act upon our beliefs?

Mattpaul then makes the following conclusion: "God has blessed us all with an awareness of ourselves and the world around us. For this reason, he calls us to work for the good of the world he created. This is our responsibility."

What do youth think about Mattpaul's conclusion?

Lesson Eleven:

Huchfee's letter of December 10th quotes Chihaysu saying of Mattpaul's death, "Perhaps someone had to die for the wrongdoings of the people of Caperston as Jesus died for the wrongdoings of the people of Earth." What do youth think about this statement? Is this possible? Before Jesus came, the Jews sacrificed animals for the atonement of sins. Is Mattpaul's death, in anyway similar to Jesus' death or to the animal sacrifices? Or is his death simply a result of inadequate supervision by the jailors?

Chihaysu later states, "every night I pray that Jesus will someday visit us in Caperston as he visited the people of Earth." How necessary is it for the Son of God to come to Caperston? Might the message of the Son of God, presented by Chihaysu, combined with the death of Mattpaul, allow believers in Caperston to be cleansed and enter the Kingdom of God? In this scenario Mattpaul's death is not a cleansing sacrifice. Rather Mattpaul's death draws attention to the teachings of Chihaysu. He is a youth so committed to the teachings that he was willing to die for them.

Lesson Twelve:

Lesson twelve is a reference. The premise to the book is that after the Big Bang, the universe, infinitely small, split into identical universes. Like identical twins, these universes evolved quite similarly yet with differences.
How do Christians deal with the Big Bang theory? The author has previously published a book entitled, "Not the Same Old, Done-it-before Youth Meetings." It is 360 pages of activity ideas for youth leaders to use in youth group meetings. Chapter 21 of the book is entitled, "Cosmology and Genesis 1 and 2." The chapter is a twelve-page explanation of the similarities and differences between the Biblical account of creation and modern theory. It includes activities for youth to help them understand that the writer of Genesis seemed to understand scientific theories better than scientists did less than 100 years ago. The similarities between the Big Bang theory and Genesis chapters one and two are striking.

If interested, the book is available through Amazon.com. More information on this topic can be obtained by contacting the author, Tim Ferguson, through his website: http://lessonsforchristianyouth.com

Appendix 3

The Story Continues with the Second Book in the Series: *New Pathways 'Cross Broken Highways*

Tensions rise among the Mountain People, who blame Pontos for Mattpaul's death. Chihaysu is unaware of this, having left for a vision quest in the desert, where he meets Princess Cle-as from Romas, the biggest city on the planet. Cle-as cannot become queen until she marries and, having heard about Chihaysu's wisdom, she wants to marry him.

He, then, has an extraordinary dream of walking in a woods where he is faced with a decision at a fork in the path. He takes the path less traveled and is immediately transported to a door with a window. Through the window he sees an unknown world. He is faced with a choice to open the door or return.

Shortly thereafter, Alex from Earth, after playing in a basketball game for the championship, has the same vision and he also chooses the path less traveled and opens the door into Caperston.

Alex becomes involved in the events taking place in Caperston and Romas assisting the believers and befriending them.

Mattpaul's father has a vision of his son asking him to believe. His father is saved with the assistance of Alex and is brought to Chihaysu. Chihaysu gives him a new name, Sa-ved. He becomes a devoted follower of Chihaysu and believer in God.

The story continues introducing the reader to the Hugapod nation. Several events are reminiscent of the challenges early Christians faced, as recorded in the book of Acts.

Eighteen months of dramatic events on Earth and in Caperston brings an unexpected conclusion for both worlds.

www.ingramcontent.com/pod-product-compliance
Lightning Source LLC
Chambersburg PA
CBHW072013170626
46813CB00005B/2135